Cover art by Brenda Walter
Editing by Heather Hayden
Narration by Jay

This is a work of fiction. Similarities to real people, places, or events are entirely coincidental.

BEST FRIENDS IN THE SHOW ME STATE PAPERBACK

First edition. July 1, 2020.

Copyright © 2020 Jessie Gussman.

Written by Jessie Gussman.

Chapter 1

"Here's the permission slip for Friday's field trip." Marlowe Glass handed the paper through the back of the pickup and over the kids and seats that were strapped there.

Her best friend, Clark Hudson, grabbed it and stuck it in his mouth, freeing both hands to shift the booster seat so he could buckle his son's seatbelt.

Marlowe was thankful Clark could take Kylie, her niece/adopted daughter, to school with his son in the mornings, so Marlowe could go to work, but, seriously? He had the permission slip in his mouth.

She lifted a brow, which Clark did not notice, at the paper now protruding from his mouth, and rolled her eyes. She should have waited until he had buckled Huck.

Her eyes shifted to Kylie, already buckled in her seat and waiting primly, her brown hair neatly pulled back in curly brown pigtails – the same color as Marlowe's shoulder length curly hair, and the color she shared with her mom, Marlowe's sister. Kylie's hands were folded in her lap, her big brown eyes watching "Uncle" Clark finish buckling his son.

"Make sure Uncle Clark holds the cupcakes levelly and doesn't bump them," Marlowe said, adjusting the cupcake holder on the floor under Kylie's feet.

"I will," Kylie said seriously.

"Do I get a cupcake?" Huck asked as the belt clicked into place. His hair was a white blond – the same color Clark's had been as a child, although it had darkened to a golden brown as he'd gotten older. They shared the same light blue eyes, too.

"Today during Kylie's birthday party, you can have one," Marlowe said as she set Kylie's backpack that contained her snack and an extra shirt in case she got a little icing on it, beside the cupcakes. It should act as a buffer in case Clark took the "shortcut" through the field roads trying to beat the bus. They were late enough this morning that he might feel like he had to.

"But you sat two on the front seat. I thought that was one for me and one for the kids to split." Clark's swirled brown eyes met hers across the kids and seats.

This time, she made sure he noticed her raised brow. "If the kids eat a cupcake on the way to school in the back of your pickup, Huck, especially, will have icing on him from his forehead to the tips of his sneakers." She smiled at Huck, just so he didn't think she thought that was necessarily a personality flaw on his part. To add an exclamation point to her smile, she said, "Because Huck is a boy, he will also manage to get icing on every exposed and unexposed surface, including his underwear." As she figured he would, Huck howled with laughter as only a five-year-old boy could. Even Kylie smiled.

The word "underwear" did it every time for a boy that age.

Still, it was the truth. Every parent knew that cupcake icing multiplied in the hands of a child. Even more so if the parent was not looking—and Clark should be driving and would definitely not be looking.

"There's not that much icing on a half a cupcake," Clark said with his own raised brow. She'd never been able to intimidate him, which was probably why they'd gotten along so well since they'd both been in diapers—his dirty, loose, and sagging on the ground, hers perfectly pinned and covered with not a speck of dirt on it.

"Clark. Your child is five. Surely you know by now that when you cut a cupcake in half the icing quadruples."

Both of Clark's brows shot up, like he seriously hadn't known it and was, far from being perturbed, actually intrigued.

"Really? The icing's the best part."

She blew a breath out—only partly in mock consternation—and put a hand up. "NO. Do not try this at home. OR on the way to delivering your child to school. I promise it will not be pretty."

"The icing is pink. The only way it isn't going to be pretty is if I don't get at least some of it in my stomach." Clark threw Huck's bookbag on the floor. It was only partially zipped, and Marlowe was pretty sure that was a three-day-old apple core that threatened to tumble out on top of what looked like dirty gym shorts and possibly a small ball of dog hair. Only...they didn't have a dog.

While Marlowe was still trying to figure out how to not strain the bonds of their best-friendship by mentioning the possibility of child services impounding the backpack, Clark reached up and across the console to snag one of the cupcakes.

"How about if I eat the icing and just give Huck the bottom?" he asked, a little grin making the dimple at the corner of his mouth pop.

"No! I want the icing!" Huck reached for the cupcake.

"Can't argue with logic like that," Clark said.

"Put that back! You can't give him a cupcake. He'll have it all over him, and you can't eat it in front of him, because that's just rude."

"Rude is a personality flaw," Clark intoned in the voice that parents everywhere use to impart timeless wisdom to their children. He split the cupcake in two. "Dirt washes off." He handed one half of the cupcake to Huck, who grabbed it eagerly, knowing, most probably, that he needed to act fast since Marlowe had been in his life from the day he was born and she was quite likely to rip the cupcake out of his hands in order to keep him clean.

He didn't want to risk losing the cupcake.

It didn't even surprise Marlowe, although it did make her heart cramp up in that yummy, good way that only Clark could instigate, that Clark leaned across the seat and offered the rest of the cupcake to Kylie.

If Kylie's eyes could lick their lips, tongues would have been out. But her little hands squeezed together, still on her lap, and her face turned to her aunt/mother.

It was times like this that Marlowe felt she was letting her late sister, Elanor, down. When Elanor and her husband and their mother had died in the car crash, Marlowe had not hesitated to take Kylie and raise and love her as her own daughter. She'd filed the papers and adopted her.

She wanted to raise Kylie perfectly, as her sister would have done.

Which meant no sugar for breakfast, no cupcakes in the car, and most definitely not allowing her little charge, who had become a daughter, to go to school with icing on her face.

But Clark's dimple flashed, and he blinked twice. Slowly. Her eyes shifted to see Kylie looking up at her—no pleading on her face, but resigned acceptance.

She nodded. "You can have it." She had to stop short of saying she didn't care if she got icing on her face or not.

Kylie's face broke out into a grin, and yes, there was a little surprise on it, too.

"Thank you!" she said, reaching for the half cupcake Clark held out.

"You keep doing stuff like that, and I'll quit thinking you're a stick-in-the-mud." Clark grabbed the other cupcake she'd put on the front seat. "You splitting this with me?"

"Of course." If only to keep him from getting the whole thing since he'd gotten her to allow Kylie to eat one before school. "If the kids get in trouble for being hyper in school, I'm telling Mrs. Barton to talk to you." They had an agreement with the school—Marlowe was the one who was called if either Kylie or Huck needed anything during the day, since Clark was often in the field or occupied on the farm. Marlowe worked for the feed mill Clark's family owned, so she could get off and be at the school in five minutes. She took a small bite of the cupcake. It was pretty good, if she did say so herself.

"They're gonna be fine. Aren't ya, kids?" Clark ruffled Huck's hair while shoving the entire half of cupcake in his mouth.

Huck nodded, florescent pink icing lining his mouth and dotting his John Deere green T-shirt.

Clark held his fist out for Kylie, and she bumped it with hers. At least she only had a couple of little spots of icing on her lips.

Marlowe took another nibble and backed out, but didn't shut the door. If she remembered correctly, she had some wet wipes in the glove box. A parent got addicted to those things when their kid was little and stockpiled them everywhere.

Maybe not every parent, she thought, throwing a glance at Clark who was making a show of licking his fingers.

"When was the last time you washed your hands?" she asked him, grabbing the wet wipes out of the glove box and slamming it shut. She set her half of the cupcake, which was mostly uneaten, on the seat.

"I'm washing 'em now," Clark said, his tongue going out and licking the next finger.

Huck grinned, showing the gap where his front two teeth were missing. "Me too."

Marlowe held one finger up. "Just wait, Kylie. I have wipes." She pushed out of the seat and hurried around the open door, leaning in to wipe her child. "You didn't get very much icing on you at all. Thanks for being careful."

She said it low, because she didn't want to make Huck feel bad, although the little guy probably didn't realize he had pink on the ribbing of his shirt, some on his arm, and somehow a bit on his shoe. The smeared, pink fingerprints on the leg of his pants were not a mystery, though. Like any kid, he'd wiped his fingers on his leg before he started to "wash" them.

She was never going to be able to get all that off him.

Taking Kylie's hand in hers, she used the wet wipe to get the sticky off.

Clark spit in his hand.

"Wait!" Marlowe said. "Here." She handed him a wet wipe, pretty sure he'd been going to use his fingers and spit to clean his son's face off.

She supposed that would work, if they were out in the woods maybe. But the kid was going to school.

Huck didn't seem to care.

"You haven't forgotten Cub Scouts after school today, right?" Clark said as he grabbed the wet wipe from her hand.

"No." She never forgot anything. She had to give Clark credit; he didn't usually forget anything either. But it didn't hurt to remind him. "Tomorrow, remember you have to leave half an hour early, because Kylie has baton practice before school."

"I got it. We're tossing the sticks around tomorrow morning." He held his fist out again, and Kylie bumped it, smiling as she did so.

Marlowe's heart did that squeezing thing again. She could not have hoped for a better best friend. Kylie loved Clark, even if he was a lot different than they were. And she and Huck got along just great. In fact, Marlowe might say that they were best friends too.

She and Clark didn't really talk about it, never had, but Kylie and Huck reminded her a lot of Clark and her when they were little. They even lived in the same houses.

But Marlowe's mother had died. And she never really lived with her dad and didn't even know where he was.

Clark's parents had moved into a big mansion they'd built outside of town. They deserved it. They worked hard all their lives and had scrimped and saved for their sons, building the feed mill business in town.

All of his brothers had moved to their own places, and Clark had bought the old farmhouse.

"Don't forget tomorrow's hat day for the whole kindergarten," Clark reminded her. "If Kylie needs a cowboy hat to borrow, she can come over and have her pick."

"Like any of your old cowboy hats would fit her."

"Mom ordered me one off the Internet, and it fits me just fine. We've had it for several weeks now, and I can't wait to wear it to school."

"Several weeks?" Clark grinned. "That sounds just like your mom." He looked across the seat, his dimple flashing.

Marlowe smiled back, of course she did. They might be as different as two people could be, but they'd learned to live with each other. Or at least respect, and sometimes even enjoy, each other's differences.

She didn't know where she would be if it hadn't been for Clark after her mom and sister had died. With Huck and Kylie, they'd struggled through diapers and bottles and birthday parties together, since it hadn't been long after that when Clark's wife had left him.

"Here's another one." She handed another wet wipe over.

"Don't need it. I think I got it all." Clark looked Huck over.

Pink icing was smeared pretty much from the top of his head to the bottom of his feet. Marlowe just smiled and shook her head.

"If you had time, I'd suggest you go change. But you're pushing it now."

"I'll take a shortcut through the fields. We'll be there in plenty of time."

"Uncle Clark almost always has us there just in time for the bell to ring as we're walking up the sidewalk." Kylie was again sitting primly, her hands folded in her lap.

Marlowe's lips pulled back in a smile. "As you're walking up the sidewalk?" Technically, that was late.

She supposed she couldn't complain though. Since he took the kids to school, she could make it to work on time and get off in time to pick them up. If he didn't do that, she would have to be late and leave early. His parents owned the feed store, and they probably wouldn't dock her pay, but she wouldn't feel right about doing it without a pay cut.

"Okay, I haven't forgotten about your boys' night out tonight. I'll have the kids home as soon as Huck's practice is over, and you're bringing supper from the diner, correct?"

"Yep. Already have it ordered. And it's not a boys' night out. That's what girls do. This is a single dad support group meeting."

Marlowe laughed outright at that. It was nothing but a bunch of guys getting together and spending the evening yakking and eating junk food. Sometimes they played pool, too. Once in a while in the summer, they went fishing. And they did it once a month.

"Really?" She had to give him a hard time. "I'm pretty sure there are other people that show up who aren't single dads."

"You've never been there, so you can't say."

"Well, you can call it what it is or call it what you want."

"Speaking of calling what it is, I'll be watching the kids tomorrow night when you go for your gossip session at the church." He grinned and winked before stepping back and slamming the door shut.

Marlowe gasped, pretty much in mock outrage, though she was a little annoyed. "It's not a gossip session," she called, in a louder voice than necessary, as he opened the driver's door and slid in the seat. "We try out new recipes and make meals for shut-ins. It's a ladies' benefit society. Just because they have pretty much gone extinct across the country doesn't mean you can't call it what it is."

She heard the snob in her voice and tried to modulate it. She had a tendency to get like that.

Bending down, careful to put an easy, sweet smile on her face, she said to Kylie, "I love you, sweetie. I hope you have a great birthday party at school today." She kissed Kylie's forehead. "And you have a good day too." She held out her fist for Huck, and he smacked it with his.

"If there are any cupcakes left, can we have them?" Huck asked, eyeing the container on the floor under Kylie's feet.

"How about we talk about that on the way home, okay?"

She'd have to think of something. She didn't really want pink icing all over the back seat of her car.

But having cupcakes as an after-school snack wouldn't hurt them once in a while, and she was almost okay with it—if she could contain the mess.

She backed out, her hand on the door. Before she closed it, she called up to Clark, "Take it easy on the turns. Don't forget about the cupcakes."

"Oh, I'm definitely not forgetting about the cupcakes. And if there's any left, I think Huck ought to have to split them with me, since I only got a half of one." Clark smirked before sticking something in his mouth that looked suspiciously like the rest of the cupcake she'd left on the front seat.

Her mouth formed an "O," but she decided to let him off the hook. She put a hand on her hip. "I made enough for you to take to your guys' gossip session tonight. They're at home on my counter. You can get them when you bring supper over."

"Hey, seriously, it looks like there's going to be some storms tonight. If you don't mind, I think it'd be better if you watch the kids at my house."

Her eyes had snapped to his as soon as he started talking about the weather. She never really paid too much attention to it, because Clark always did. And he would take care of her, she knew.

They each had their areas. The weather was his. She made sure the kids got to their dentist appointments and doctors' appointments, and she kept both of their shot records too.

Clark was a farmer, along with his family owning the feed mill, so the weather was definitely his area.

His eyes were serious; the swirled brown had deepened and darkened. She loved his easy laugh and his easier-going personality. But she also loved that he knew how to be responsible. This was one of those times. She only needed a second to look at his face to know that he was dead serious.

Sometimes the storms didn't materialize, but it could be deadly to assume that they weren't going to.

"Okay. I'll bring them to my house, we'll get changed, and then we'll pack up some stuff and head over to yours. If you're as late as you were last month, you might have a girl sleeping over again."

"That's fine. We have a couple spare rooms, and she can take her pick."

"Yay!" Kylie shouted from the back. "I want Chandler's old room. He's got dinosaur bones in it."

Marlowe had forgotten about that. Chandler was so good looking, and such a successful movie actor, that she kinda forgot he had a brain sometimes.

"It's yours, kid." He looked back at Marlowe. "And you're welcome to stay on the couch again if you want. Or I can try to be earlier."

"No," she said immediately. He hardly ever got out, just this once-a-month gathering. She certainly didn't want him to cut short the one evening that he actually took off each month. When things got busy in the spring and fall, he might not even make it. "You can be as late as you want. I'll bring a few clothes and plan on sleeping on the couch."

"We'll just be in the back room of the feed mill. It's only a mile away. I'll keep an eye on the weather, so you don't have to worry about it."

She gave him a smile, and he grinned at her. They both knew, of all the things she worried about, she didn't worry about the weather. She supposed she should. Cowboy Crossing was located front and center in tornado alley, being as it was in Missouri.

Everyone in Missouri paid attention to the weather come springtime.

"Okay. You want me to admit that you have me spoiled. I admit it. I don't worry about the weather."

"You're the only person in Missouri who doesn't. Especially this time of year."

"Fine." She slapped the roof of the car. "You want me to admit it. I don't have a problem with that. That's because you do it for me."

"Relax, Low Beam. You don't have to get all huffy about it."

She rolled her eyes at her nickname. She couldn't even remember how he gave it to her. But she had one for him, and she broke it out. "I am relaxed, Gable. You're the one that was trying to rub it in, and we both know why I don't pay attention to the weather."

He grinned at her use of his nickname. They both knew how he got it, although neither one of them probably remembered exactly where or when she'd first seen *Gone with the Wind* and started calling him Clark Gable instead of Clark Hudson. Eventually, she had shortened it to just Gable, only using it when he called her Low Beam.

His eyes were smiling, but there was a little bit of a cloud in there, and she knew he was probably worried about her.

Watching the weather stressed her. Which was why she didn't do it. He was one of the few who knew it. They never really talked about it anyway. She'd actually never told him; he'd just seen her have a panic attack once as she'd walked through the room where he had been watching the weather. From that point on, he made a point of making sure that she knew he'd watch it for her, and he let her know if she needed to know anything.

She didn't worry about the weather exactly; there was just something about watching people talk about it on TV, especially bad weather coming, that scared her.

Half the time, the weather people were wrong anyway. No point in being scared unnecessarily.

Clark could handle it.

"Keep an eye on your cell phone. The weather is not supposed to come until this evening sometime after supper. If it comes at all."

"Can we stand outside and watch the lightning, Dad?" Huck asked.

Clark's guilty look clashed with her accusing one. She crossed her arms over her chest, and she knew her look was saying, *yeah, that's real safe.*

She didn't say anything, though, because she didn't want to scare Huck.

"Okay, you guys be safe." She tapped her hand on the roof of his pickup once more, blew an air kiss to Kylie, and waved at Huck before shutting the door.

Clark didn't waste any time before driving away. She watched him go, knowing, although he was very different than her and wouldn't be as careful as she, her child could be in no better hands.

Chapter 2

Clark pulled into his house, late.

Marlowe would understand. She'd grown up around farmers and ranchers, and she knew all about working while the sun shone. So all he'd have to do would be to tell her that the planter broke down, and he had to spend three hours fixing it, then mention the rain that was coming this evening, and she'd know exactly why he was late. He'd needed to get things done and as much corn in the ground as he could before it got too wet to work.

Still, he knew it wasn't easy to be at home with two hungry five-year-olds. He hated that he'd done that to Marlowe. Although, of course, he'd texted her to let her know.

She could've gone into the diner and picked up the food, but he hadn't really thought about it and she didn't suggest it.

Slamming the pickup door shut, he walked around the other side to get the take-out containers that were sitting on the floor. The wind blew, rattling the leaves in the big old oak that stood between his house and hers.

His home was the old farmhouse, the original one on the property, although her home was almost as old, but only half as big. It had been deeded off the farm at some point in its history.

Her family had lived in it all his life. After her mother and sister had died in the car accident, Marlowe had used the life insurance money to pay down the mortgage then had taken over the rest of the payments. She'd just paid it off last year.

Another gust of wind blew, and he glanced up at the budding leaves on the oak tree as he started up the walk. Bright green and pretty, they still weren't full-size, but they waved in the strong spring wind.

He and his brothers, along with Marlowe and her sister Elanor, had built a makeshift treehouse in that tree and climbed it for years.

He looked at the one branch that leaned way over her house. When they were about seven, they'd each had their first kiss there. They'd both hated it; she'd even spit and almost pushed him off the tree. To be honest, he wasn't any more impressed with her kissing ability.

Kind of laughed at the thought.

They hadn't exactly had a verbal agreement from that time on to just be friends, but that was what had happened.

Marlowe had grown into a beautiful woman. Although she was definitely bossy and a control freak. If a guy could live with that, he'd have a pretty, bossy control freak as a wife. But she hadn't found anyone that gullible yet.

He chuckled, knowing he wasn't really being serious with himself. Marlowe would make any man a wonderful wife.

The empty plastic bucket he used to water the plants skidded across the porch as a stronger gust of wind puffed across the yard.

He couldn't believe the bucket had made it through the winter. He made a mental note to pick it up sometime when he had hands.

He was just about to bang his elbow on the door when it opened. "My goodness, it's getting windy out. Come on in here." Marlowe stood in jeans and a pink shirt, her hair in a ponytail and her face scrubbed clean, holding both doors open.

"She's still just as bossy as she ever was."

"If you're not nice to me, I'll take the food and shut the door in your face."

"This is my house. We forgot that?"

"Regardless of whose house it is, you still have to be nice to me. You can go to my house. I have the kids here."

"I wasn't being unkind. I just simply stated the fact. You're still bossy."

"Everyone knows bossiness is not an appealing character trait. And I'm working on it. The very least you can do is be kind."

"Be kind? You want me to lie?"

She huffed a breath, and he chuckled as she pulled the screen door shut behind him and then closed the solid door with a snap.

"Where are the kids? I thought they would attack me when I came in. I'm sorry about being late."

"I gave them some flour and water and food coloring, and they're down in the cellar doing experiments."

"Whoa. They're liable to get dirty."

"It's okay if they get dirty now. They're not on their way to school."

She followed him back down the hall to the kitchen where he set the stuff on the table.

"I had to do something to keep them occupied. They're starving." There was a pause, which made him turn. She had a little grin tripping around the corners of her mouth. That never boded well. "I had to give them your cupcakes."

"My cupcakes? The ones you promised me?" He tried to keep his voice from squeaking, but he couldn't contain his dismay.

She looked over her shoulder. "Yep. I had no choice. The kids were starving. I understand that the corn planter broke and that you had to finish planting before you could quit. But they didn't. At least their stomachs didn't. Although, once their stomachs had cupcakes in them, they were *much* more understanding."

"Are you trying to tell me that you fed my child cupcakes for supper?"

"I guess you've influenced me after all, haven't you?"

He would've laughed, because he knew she was joking. But he was actually kind of worried.

Were there really no cupcakes?

"Did you not even save me one back?" He had half of one this morning, and it was about the best cupcake he'd ever eaten. Marlowe could cook like sixty.

Her dream, once upon a time, had been to go to college. He was pretty sure she wasn't going to culinary school, but she'd been interested in chemistry. He had no idea what kind of job someone with a chemistry degree could get. Maybe they had to get another degree to go with their chemistry degree in order to get a job. That's probably the kind of degree it was. But still, Marlowe could be so much more than just the clerk at the feed store. But she'd given it all up for her sister and for Kylie.

"You're looking very sad, Gable."

"Something about the cupcakes that I didn't get to eat. It would make any man sad."

He would never tell her he'd been thinking about the college education she didn't get. She'd blow that off anyway, and she definitely wouldn't want to be told about it. She didn't consider it a sacrifice. She considered it a duty. An honorable duty, he supposed.

But if she hadn't given up her college education, she'd probably have come back married. Or maybe she wouldn't have come back at all. But she would've been married. There's no way she could have made it through four years of college without having some guy snap her up.

Her honey blond hair cascaded in her ponytail, and the ends danced between her shoulder blades.

She set the bags down on the table and turned, looking at him under her lashes. "Did you get me an eggplant Parmesan sub with ranch dressing, mushrooms, and spinach?"

One side of his lips tilted up. "Maybe." He tried to keep his lips from breaking into a grin. "What's in it for me if I did?"

"Oh, I don't know. Maybe, just maybe, I could remember that I hid half a dozen cupcakes somewhere." She tapped her chin with her first finger. "The location is coming to me. I just need to hear you say the right words."

"I'm sorry, but eggplant Parmesan with ranch dressing, mushrooms, and spinach is just gross. I couldn't order that if you paid me to."

"You've ordered it before."

"And I almost got run out of town. People think you're weird when you eat like that."

"No," she said, sticking her tongue out at him. "People think *you* are weird when I eat like that. Because you order it."

"Exactly. I have a reputation to uphold in this town. I can't have people looking at me like I'm some weirdo from out east."

"You've just insulted millions of people."

"No, I didn't. I just insulted one weirdo. From out east."

"The insinuation is that people from out east are weird. Just because they're not like you does not mean that they're weird."

"I didn't say that. I just said the weirdo, that people think I am, comes from out east. Which is obviously where all weird things come from."

"See? You did it again. There are millions of people who are offended at you right now."

He shook his head. For being such a straight-laced, punctual, almost-OCD person, Marlowe could be a real goofball. Maybe that was how they had managed to get along for so long. Because she didn't take herself too seriously. And she definitely didn't take him seriously. "Listen, I'll apologize to every single one of them if you manage to remember where you put the cupcakes."

He walked over to the oven and opened the door. That was her go-to spot. It was empty.

"You're not gonna find them. You might as well stop looking."

"I found them before. Just give me time."

"You found something I hid, exactly one time, when we were ten and Chandler didn't close his eyes while you guys were supposed to be counting, and he told you where they were. That's not a very good track record."

"My lucky streak is just about to start. Today."

"Tell me you got me the eggplant Parmesan sandwich with ranch dressing and mushrooms and spinach. That's all you have to do."

"I told you. I have a reputation to uphold in this town. I can't even say that without people starting to whisper about locking me in the tower."

Marlowe crossed her arms over her chest and tapped her toe. The pink shirt she wore made her gray eyes look green. Sometimes they would turn blue depending on her outfit. And they definitely could flash and snap with temper, although not nearly the way they used to. She'd grown into a pretty even-tempered person.

His stomach rumbled, he was dirty, and he still needed to shower before he could leave. He figured he'd teased her long enough.

"I got you the sandwich that you wanted. It's in the bag. It would be easy for you to look for yourself."

"I just want you to tell me."

"I ordered it, eggplant Parmesan, with ranch dressing, which is gross by the way, with mushrooms and spinach. No one in their right mind would like that, let alone eat it. But go get it, since that's what's in the bag sitting on my table."

Her smile was smug, and she blinked her eyes. "Your cupcakes are in the garbage can."

His jaw dropped. "You're kidding."

"Nope."

He narrowed his eyes, looking at her. She looked like she was telling the truth. Marlowe never lied. Although she would tease him to death and back, on occasion. He hoped that this was one of those occasions.

"Well, you're right about one thing, I definitely would never have thought to look there."

If possible, her smile got even more smug. "Didn't think so, which is why I put them there."

He tried to remember when the last time was he'd emptied the garbage can.

"I hope you had them in some kind of container."

"No. There's no way I'm gonna throw my good container away."

She sounded serious about that too.

He took two steps toward the garbage can before her voice stopped him. "Gable, I cannot believe that you believe me. Really? You seriously think I would put the cupcakes in the garbage can? That is disgusting." He looked up at her, and she was shaking her head. "No. What is actually disgusting is that you were really going to go over to the garbage can, and get the cupcakes out, and eat them. That's what's really disgusting."

Okay. He could see what was going on here. "You knew I was going to make fun of you for the disgusting sandwich that you always order. So you had to devise a way to make fun of me for being disgusting. Am I right?"

She bit her lip, and her shoulders drooped. "Too juvenile?"

He flattened his lips and nodded. "Wish I'da thought of it first."

She lifted her lip a little. "I really didn't think about it until we were in the kitchen and you were looking in the oven and I saw the garbage can. It was a spur-of-the-moment thing."

"It's your inner child coming out, then?"

"You didn't know I had one of those?"

"I have to admit she did surprise me. I haven't seen it for a while. That inner child."

She walked over to the refrigerator, opened the door, moved a gallon of milk and two dozen eggs, and pulled out the cupcakes that were hidden behind it. "These are all yours. I did give the kids a couple, but there should still be enough for you to take tonight. Depending on how many guys are going to be there."

"There's never more than a dozen or so of us."

"Well, there's two dozen there. Twenty-three if you eat one before you go." She laughed. "Which I assume you're going to do."

"Hey, these have blue icing."

"Well, yeah. I could hardly send two dozen cupcakes that were decorated in pink icing to the guys' gossip night."

He loved that about her. She'd been planning on sending cupcakes with him all along and had made these especially for it.

"People say you're a hard woman, but they don't know you like I do."

"Shut up." She snapped the dish towel off the refrigerator handle and threw it at his head.

He caught it easily, reaching out, taking the cupcakes out of her hands, and draping the dish towel over her face. "Now that's a pretty good look if I do say so myself. Anytime you want help with your wardrobe, just ask."

"Yeah. I'll get right on that." She yanked the towel off and rolled her eyes. "If I'd ever needed you to dress me, we would not have remained best friends."

"Do you think I have time to take a shower before you call the kids up?" He set the cupcakes down on the table, opened the container up, and took one out. Sure, the guys would rip him because there was a cupcake missing out of the 24-space container, but he didn't care. In fact, he thought as he took a big bite, it was better than he remembered from this morning, and he might have to eat two.

"I'm sure that we're fine. I actually let them eat two cupcakes apiece. Which I shouldn't have done, but I felt bad after they were only able to have half a cupcake this morning."

"That one, then they had a cupcake at the party. And then they had two tonight. So my child had three and half cupcakes today, all because of you."

"Are you in the shower yet?" She reached for the bag he'd brought from the diner and started pulling the containers out. "If you're not nice to me, we might not have any food left for you when you come back down."

"Why is it always about me being nice to you? When is this relationship gonna reciprocate, and you're gonna start being nice to me?" he asked as he walked out of the kitchen.

"I can't be nice to you," she called as he started up the stairs. "Every time I start being nice to you, you start trying to set me up with one of your buddies. I don't want anyone from your male gossip group. I want a man who has better things to do with his time than hang out with his buds and talk about the weather."

"We do more than talk about the weather," he called when he reached the top of the stairs. He peered into Chandler's old room, just to make sure that everything was in order for Kylie this evening. He wasn't the greatest housekeeper in the world, and sometimes he forgot to make the bed and wash the sheets. But he had done that after she left the last time, and everything looked good. "We talk about the single girls in town too," he hollered over the banister as he continued on down to his own room.

"I did not need to know that," she called up, her voice fading. He grinned, hating to give her the last word but figuring she could have it. This time.

He wished he'd been a bit more careful when he picked out his wife. He and Marlowe had been buds forever, so when he and Dana had met, and Dana was the opposite of everything Marlowe was, he thought he'd found a gem.

She wasn't hard to fall in love with. She was beautiful and everything else that Marlowe wasn't.

Agreeable, for one. Not bossy. Never bossy. She agreed with everything he said. Then she went on ahead and did her own thing. He'd call her sneaky, but she wasn't even that. She didn't try to hide what she was going to do; she just did it. She didn't try to tell him what to do. It was almost like she expected them to get married and then live separate lives.

He didn't have room in his life for regrets, and he tried to stop thinking about her. He wasn't still in love with her, though he supposed he had been at one time. Infatuated anyway. He supposed if he'd truly been in love with her, real love, it would have lasted, even after she left him. But he wasn't sure.

He'd kinda been joking about the guys talking about all the single women in town. They really didn't. Marlowe would be bored stiff, because they actually talked about tractors and planting, and they really did talk about the weather, sometimes they talked about their pickups, and at certain times of the year they definitely talked about hunting and fishing as well. He supposed there was a little bit of gossip that went around, but not much. Most of them really were single dads, and even though it really was a boys' night out, they'd talk about parenting sometimes as well.

He never thought he'd be a single dad. He certainly wouldn't have gotten married if he'd known that was what was going to happen, no matter how infatuated he was. Huck deserved to have a mom.

Grabbing some clean clothes, he threw his phone on the bed and walked over to the bathroom, determined to look ahead, not behind.

Chapter 3

By nine o'clock, Marlowe had given the children baths and supper, helped them clean up the mess that they'd made in the cellar, and snuggled down to read stories with them on the couch.

The wind picked up, and she'd heard it howling across the fields outside. There was the one big oak tree between their houses, but other than that, everything was pretty much open.

Around seven o'clock, Clark had texted and said he was keeping an eye on things and she didn't need to worry.

They were close enough to town to hear Cowboy Crossing's tornado siren, and Clark wouldn't be out if there was any danger of it going off.

She tucked both children in bed. They were sleepier than usual, probably because of their upended schedule. It wasn't completely unusual for them to be staying at one another's house, but they didn't typically do it on a school night.

She was pretty sure the guys had decided to get together tonight because it was supposed to rain, and most of them had jobs that were dependent on the weather. It's just the way it was in rural Missouri.

She turned all the lights off in the house, except the bathroom light upstairs and the kitchen light downstairs.

It was odd that she got so upset about watching the weather forecast on TV but the actual weather itself didn't upset her any more than anyone else.

Although tonight, the wind just had a different sound to it.

Any normal person would have that curl of fear in their stomach, as she did. She tried to look out the kitchen window, but it was too dark to see anything. Unable to sit still, she walked to the living room and looked out that window.

Clark's house was brick, and it had a basement. It felt, and was, much more solid than her house.

Her home was well-made but had obviously, at some point in the past history on the farm, been made for a son or daughter, or maybe even a hired hand. It didn't have the grandeur of this house.

It wasn't brick either.

She took a deep breath, blowing out, trying to think of something that would take her mind off what was going on outside.

She didn't need to worry. The tornado siren would let them know if something was going to happen.

Hopefully.

Tempted to go to the cellar and walk around, checking things out down there, she worried that she might not hear the siren.

From experience, she knew the siren was loud enough to wake the dead, and it was an unnecessary worry, but she didn't go down. Maybe she just couldn't put two stories between herself and her children. Not that Huck was hers. He just felt like it. He wasn't even a year old when Clark's wife had walked.

She couldn't imagine what would possess a woman to leave Clark. Sure, he was a little unorganized, and he enjoyed teasing, but he was about as perfect as a guy could get.

Dana had been blessed, and she'd thrown it away. That, and she'd walked away from her little boy. Unbelievable.

At the time, Don at the diner had said, "At least she didn't drown them in the bathtub like that other woman did."

Marlowe figured it was probably a blessing, because if Dana had drowned Huck in the bathtub, Clark would've drowned Dana along with him. The man had been in love with his child since the day he was born.

She admired that and was proud to be his friend.

There was a lot about Clark to admire, and she'd always been proud to be able to walk beside him and have people know that they were best friends. She liked hearing people talk about them together.

She shifted a little with that, because she remembered back when she was in ninth grade at a slumber party, she and five of her girlfriends had voted Clark as the boy in their class with the most kissable lips.

Funny, since that night, she had a little secret fantasy about Clark and kissing him. Not that she had any seriously romantic feelings about him. She'd never been the slightest bit upset when he got married. She'd supported him and Dana, even if she hadn't exactly been around for it much. Since they got married when she was a sophomore in college, the year before her mother and sister died.

She hadn't been jealous to see them together. She'd come back when her sister had died, and she had a newborn to take care of. Not long after that, Clark had a baby of his own to take care of too, with his wife spending more and more time away until she finally left for good and filed for divorce.

Marlowe passed the front door and peered out. Even the road was deserted, not that it was that busy at this time of night anyway. They were a small town, not much happening.

Especially on a night like tonight.

So yeah, she might harbor some little thoughts about Clark and his lips, and she definitely loved him better than she loved anyone else in the world, but it wasn't a romantic love.

She stood at the living room window peering out into the backyard when she thought she heard a truck motor. Hurrying to the door, she was just in time to see Clark, leaning against the wind, walking up the walk.

She opened the door and he blew in, almost losing the screen door as the wind caught it and ripped it unexpectedly.

"Boy, am I glad to see you." She hadn't thought she was that worried, but she could hear the note of fear in her voice sounding loud and clear.

Clark smiled and ruffled her hair as he finished walking in, and she closed the door behind him. She wasn't fooled by his smile; there were worry lines tightening his eyes.

"What?" She touched his sleeve. "Is it going to get that bad?"

He turned, the half-smile on his face still, but his eyes drew together. "How can you read my face so easily? I thought I was doing a really good job of just looking happy."

"I can see the worry lines clear as day. What's going on?"

He jerked his chin, and she knew he wasn't going to hide anything from her. Which was nice. She was an adult, even if she did have more of a tendency to worry than he did. He knew she could handle it, and she appreciated him letting her.

"There's a pretty severe line of storms coming. They were about half an hour away when I left the mill, heading this way pretty fast. I'm sure the siren will go off if we need it, but I'm checking my phone too. It's a little behind the actual weather, so I don't want to wait until it says they're here." He smiled, probably trying to ease the worry on her face. "We can see the storms are weakening. They usually do after dark."

She knew that. Typically, once the sun went down and things started cooling off, any thunderstorms would putter out overnight. But that wasn't always the case. And it had been unusually hot today. She didn't watch the weather, obviously, so she wasn't sure on the specifics, but today felt like a day that was conducive to night storms. It was probably more of an intuitive thing having lived in the Midwest all her life.

She crossed her arms over her chest and tried not to pace.

"I'm here now. If you'd like to lie down or go read a book, I'll make sure we get to the cellar if we need to. In fact, for this one storm, I might feel better if we just head on down when they get a little closer."

Marlowe gasped, and she felt her eyes fly wide open. It must be pretty bad, if Clark was suggesting they do that. "Have you talked to your family? Are your brothers okay?"

Clark nodded.

Marlowe's hands twisted together in front of her; she barely realized she was doing it. Her immediate family was gone, and she didn't know where her dad was. Her grandparents were also dead. She had cousins and such a few towns over, but no one to check on.

Clark's family was her family.

"Are you sure they're okay? Did you talk to your parents?"

Clark shoved his phone in his pocket and turned toward her fully, taking his hands and setting them on her shoulders. Even though they'd been friends forever, they didn't really have a touchy-feely relationship. The contact was unexpected. But welcome. She loved the weight of his hands and the warmth. Even before he opened his mouth, she felt more grounded and settled.

"Hey." His voice was warm and deep, with even a little bit of humor. If anyone could downplay a tornado, it would be Clark. But still, the fact that his voice sounded so normal calmed her even more. "This is one of those times that we put boots on our faith, roll up the sleeves, and put it to work."

Oh boy. He was right. And his words hit her straight on her forehead.

"You're right. I've been sitting here worrying and praying."

"One of those things is worthless, and one is priceless. Let's do the priceless one."

She nodded. She never even told Clark about her little rift with the Lord. They were still on speaking terms, and she still prayed. But He'd really messed up her life when her mother and sister died. Not only having to go through losing them—that was bad enough. But she'd given up everything she'd ever wanted to come back and raise Kylie.

It wasn't that she didn't love her niece who'd become a daughter officially, since she'd adopted her, because she did. She loved her. But it was more that she was still a little upset with the Lord for asking her to give up everything else.

And yeah, she knew she could have gone back to school and had someone watch the baby for her, but it just felt like cheating to not do it herself. Or maybe it just felt like she hadn't been putting her all into it, which was what she felt she owed her sister and her mom.

She closed her eyes as Clark, with his hands still on her shoulders, murmured a prayer. She prayed along. She knew God was good. She just didn't always see it.

And yeah, maybe she still had a little resentment in her heart because her life didn't go the way she wanted it to.

She kept her head bowed as Clark prayed for safety, and calm, and peace for them in their town and their families.

By the time he was done, she felt strengthened and encouraged, but she probably could blame that on Clark as much as God.

"I think we need to get the kids to the cellar," Clark said as soon as he'd said "amen."

"Now?" she asked, even though he hadn't stuttered and she heard him quite clearly. It just wasn't the thirty minutes that he had said earlier.

"Yeah. I just have a feeling about it."

She didn't want to waste time arguing, Clark didn't usually live by his feelings. Neither did she. They certainly both knew people who did. But it wasn't something that most of their community did. Reality was much more dependable than feelings.

"I'll get Kylie first."

She could kiss his feet. She knew he loved Kylie like his own daughter. And he was going by the ladies-first rule, as he always did.

"There are some blankets in the chest right over there. You grab those and carry them downstairs. You know where we always go."

She didn't say anything but ran to the chest he'd pointed to and grabbed the blankets. When she turned around, he was gone. She hurried down the steep steps to the cellar, hitting the light switch, which didn't illuminate much aside from the steps, with her elbow on the way down, careful not to fall. The last thing she needed was to be huddled in the basement with a broken leg and scared children.

The floor was dirt, but the walls around her were block; she was pretty sure the entire thing was under the ground. It's where they used to keep their vegetables in the winter to keep them from spoiling.

She'd spread a blanket on the ground and had one ready to wrap around Kylie when Clark came through the doorway with her in his arms.

This was not the first time she'd been woken up in the middle of the night and carried to safety. Every time before, nothing had happened. So when Marlowe sat down and Clark settled Kylie in Marlowe's arms, Kylie just snuggled deeper and was snoring before Clark's footsteps echoed up the cellar steps.

It was barely another minute before Clark came back with Huck. Even though Huck was usually borderline hyper, he was peaceful and still in Clark's arms as Clark came through the door and closed it behind him.

"Holy smokes, it's dark in here," Clark mumbled as the door latched.

"No windows," Marlowe whispered. "The darkness is a good thing. As in it protects us." She said that more to convince herself, since Clark already knew it, and because when the door shut and the light had gone out, her heart had jumped and twisted, taking her stomach with it. They still hadn't settled back in their rightful places.

"I'm over here. You can follow my voice."

"Keep talking."

"It sounds like you're in the middle of the room, so you need to turn a little bit maybe. I'm over here, right here." She kept talking until she felt his boot against her leg. "That's my leg. I think you can sit down right here beside me."

He put a hand out, touching her head.

There must've been a big gust of wind just then, because the noise seemed to grow between them, filling the room and the darkness with unspeakable fear.

Clark settled beside her, his warmth and presence comforting but still not containing her terror.

"That sounds terrifying. I wish we could drown it out." Another blast seemed to shake the house around them, and Kylie stirred in her arms. It'd be awful if the kids woke up. She was having enough trouble containing her own terror.

She'd barely said it when Clark began singing. Not loud, but close enough to her ear that his voice overpowered the other sounds she heard.

A wonderful Savior is Jesus my Lord.
A wonderful savior is He.
He hideth my soul in the cleft of the rock
Where rivers of pleasure I see.

His voice had grown louder as he went through the verse, not loud enough to wake the children but strong and comforting.

She'd never been able to sing like him, but she joined him in harmony on the chorus.

He hideth my soul in the cleft of the rock
That shadows a dry, thirsty land;
He hideth my life in the depths of His love,
And covers me there with His hand,
And covers me there with His hand.

Chapter 4

Clark hadn't really meant to start singing. It had been a natural response to Marlowe's fear and his own. But he was glad he had.

There was just something about music. It worked for Paul and Silas in the jail and was working for Marlowe and him in the cellar. Not to mention, he could feel Huck's little body relaxing against him, maybe from the vibrations in his chest, although more probably from the familiar music. It also drowned out the awful noise of the wind outside.

Thankfully, having been in church all his life, he knew most of the words to the verses, and what he stumbled over, Marlowe remembered.

That was one of the really nice things about Marlowe. She filled in the gaps of his weaknesses, and she did it without making a big fuss about it. Together, they made a great team.

They'd sung about three hymns when a crash that even their music couldn't cover echoed down through the cellar.

Marlowe jerked and quit singing. He quit as well, cocking his head and listening. It was close, but he was thinking it wasn't their house. At least the wind scuttling across the floor hadn't changed, and he hadn't felt any moving of the structure. Surely if something had happened to the house, they would feel it in this room, even if they wouldn't be hurt.

"What do you think that was?" Marlowe whispered next to him.

"I don't think it matters. We're alive, and our kids are safe. Let's keep singing." He didn't give her a chance to respond but started singing "Nearer My God to Thee," which as soon as he started it, he thought was a bad choice, since it was what the musicians on the Titanic had been playing as the Titanic sank.

Still, there was no denying the comfort in the words, and Marlowe created beautiful harmony with him.

After a few lines of song, she snuggled closer, and he took his arm off his son and put it around Marlowe's shoulders, pulling her close to him without breaking off his song.

Somehow, it seemed imperative, maybe for his own sanity, but for the children also, to hear the music. Or maybe it was for Marlowe. Normally she was cool and collected, although she might fuss about things he didn't think were important.

They'd somehow seemed to accept each other's differences. Accept, and maybe even respect.

He didn't like to see her upset.

His fear wasn't gone, necessarily. But he had to admit it felt good and right to have Marlowe beside him, their children on their laps cuddled up under a blanket as they sang to the Lord.

Minus the tornado, this would make a good family night. He chuckled a little.

"What?" Marlowe didn't exactly lean away from him, but she did lift her head up from his shoulder where it had been lying. "Are you...laughing?"

The hymn he was singing stumbled to a stop.

"Maybe." His hand rubbed lightly up and down her upper arm. Man, he hadn't realized how thin she was. She seemed like such a sturdy, capable person.

"We are in a dangerous, life-threatening situation, and you were laughing? Now I've heard everything." She shook her head. In the darkness, he could feel her hair brush against his neck.

"Okay. I can understand you being upset at my perceived lack of maturity and seriousness. But isn't it better that I'm laughing rather than crying?"

She snorted.

Yeah, that's what he thought.

"You've got me there. Laugh away, my friend."

"I'd like it better if you were laughing with me."

"I was singing with you. I'm sure if you start laughing, you'll end up dragging me along with that too."

"You were enjoying the singing."

"You're right. It's been a long time since we sang together. We used to do it all the time in, what, junior high?"

"Yeah. That was back when you were thinking you were going to Hollywood like my brother Chandler. You dragged me along as your supporting man. Today, you were the one singing harmony."

She laughed, softly, but maybe it was a testament to the stress of the evening, because she didn't give him a smart comment back. "I always loved to hear you sing." She paused, then continued. "Your voice sounds a little different now than it did in junior high."

He could hear the smile in her voice. And he realized that the danger had probably passed, although neither one of them was thinking about it anymore. Funny how music and a conversation with a friend could pass the time so pleasantly, even in such circumstances.

Friend.

He needed to remember that, because it had become very easy for him to sit here in the dark and look at Marlowe like she was...more.

Like a wife.

Like they were family.

Maybe they could be a family, in their patched-up, convoluted way, but Marlowe was most definitely not his wife.

Clark realized his hand had been rubbing up and down her upper arm for quite some time, and he had been enjoying it. Enjoying that, and the closeness of her body, and the scent that was all hers, deep and pure and no-nonsense just like she was, with just a touch of sweetness and sparkle. He couldn't even put a name on it. But when he smelled it, he knew exactly who it was. It was unique to her.

He supposed his lapse was understandable, because a storm like this wasn't an everyday occurrence, but he needed to be more careful. His friendship with Marlowe was lifelong and very strong. But she was a very straightforward kind of person. If he made a pass at her, their friendship would be ruined.

He'd realized it already in some ways, but tonight had made it clear that she was beautiful and desirable and womanly. However, it couldn't negate the fact that she was also his best friend and totally off-limits for him in that area.

No matter how perfect it might be for them to join their families together.

He shifted, drawing his hand away from around her and dropping it on his son, rubbing over Huck's head and down his shoulder. In the dark, Marlowe couldn't see, but hopefully she would assume he pulled his arm away to check his kid and not because he was uncomfortable and feeling like he was crossing a line.

"I think it might be over," he said softly.

When he pulled his arm away, she straightened, their thighs still touching but their upper bodies separated. He missed the warmth and the softness. He appreciated the trust that she placed in him by curling up beside him and putting her life and the life of her child in his hands. He maybe didn't deserve the trust, but he loved it.

"I think you might be right." Her head seemed to shift in the darkness, and he missed the soft touch of her hair against his neck when it did so. "I almost want to stay here. Not sure what it's going to look like out there, and that's scary."

"Let me see if I can get out from underneath Huck. I'll go out and check. Just before I came down, I tried to send a text, but it wouldn't go through. I'm not sure if maybe a cell phone tower was down or something...."

"You can say, 'I didn't want to scare you and make an already bad situation worse.'" She grunted a little laugh, and he was grateful for her attempt at levity. That was exactly what he'd thought. Of course, she knew it. "We'll deal," she added.

"It might have just been a temporary interruption. Maybe the system was overloaded or something."

He shifted, and her hand came out, brushing his.

Over the years, he'd touched Marlowe a million times. Goofing off, ruffling her hair, smacking her arm, grasping her hand to pull her up a tree, or having her shove him off the side of the pool into the deep end of the water. Lots of times, all the time.

So he froze for a moment when her hand brushed his and his skin tingled, sending little shockwaves up his arm and into his heart.

He'd already decided he could not allow himself to ruin what they had. With his odd feelings of family, and his enjoyment of her heat and scent and that softness, and now this tingle thing.

He must have been more scared than he thought he was. Although he knew he had been plenty scared. It was all the aftereffects of the fierce storm.

He managed to only hesitate for a fraction of a second before he continued to slide out from under Huck. Marlowe helped, and by the time Clark stood up, Huck's head and shoulders were lying on Marlowe, squeezed in between her stomach and Kylie.

Just as he had gone up to get Kylie first, he knew Marlowe would defend his son with her life. Although he was pretty sure the danger was over.

Pulling a cell phone out, he switched the flashlight app on, pointing it down toward the floor.

"Are you okay if I go look around?" he asked, low, careful not to wake the kids.

"Yes." There was a slight hesitation before she spoke, and her voice sounded odd in the darkness, not quite as confident. "Please don't go far."

His eyes shot to hers. Again, he wasn't used to Marlowe not being totally in control or at least trying to be in control. He didn't mind, and he even liked having her depend on him. It definitely made him want to be more. He didn't want her to be disappointed.

Which was definitely a new feeling, because he never worried about that before either. She was his best friend; of course she wasn't going to be disappointed in him.

"I won't. If I'm going to be out of shouting distance, I'll come back to let you know. I just want to make sure we can get out of our house. That the house is even still there."

Obviously, the house was still partially there, because the roof was still on the room that they were in. But there had definitely been a lot of crashing going on, and he was afraid of what he might find when he walked out.

"Clark?" Marlowe's voice was even softer with even more hesitation and insecurity in it.

He almost didn't want to answer her. Pretend he hadn't heard. He was afraid of what she was going to ask. And he didn't even know why.

He couldn't do that to her. "Yeah?"

"Please...please, be careful."

Up until that point, he assumed that the heat and the softness and the tingles were all him. Products of the storm and fear, of course, but all him. With that slight hesitation and insecure note in her voice, that pleading almost, he wondered if maybe she felt a little of that, too.

That the storm had affected them both that way.

And suddenly he worried that their relationship might have shifted. That whatever was outside destroyed by the tornado was only an outward manifestation of the inward shift and possible destruction that had happened between them this evening, tonight, in the dark in the cellar.

Or Marlowe had gone from being his best friend and slipped away from him just a little, because neither one of them could go down that path. That path of attraction. Because that's what it felt like.

"I will." He meant it, too. Because if anything happened to him, his family of course would take care of Marlowe, but she would be completely alone in the world. He didn't want that for her. She'd already been through enough.

He grabbed the latch on the door—it didn't have a knob like a regular door—and lifted it, pulling.

He shone his phone around, not sure what he expected, but everything looked normal.

"Looks good out here. I'm going to the steps and walking up."

"You promised."

She did not need to remind him of his promise; he knew exactly what he'd said. He'd be careful.

He walked slowly, because he wasn't sure about the structure of the house. He assumed everything was okay. Everything looked the same as it had an hour ago. Was it even an hour? The storm probably hadn't lasted that long. They talked and sang, and time flew by without them even realizing it.

He reached the cellar steps and carefully went up. There seemed to be some kind of heavy anticipation in the air. Maybe anticipation was the wrong word. Heavy foreboding. Like in a horror movie before the murderer showed up.

He shook that feeling, finished climbing the stairs, and pushed the door open.

Again, it felt anticlimactic as he shone his cell phone flashlight around the kitchen. Nothing had changed. Everything was exactly the way it had been when he had shut the door behind him and run down the stairs with Huck.

He turned around and called down the cellar steps, "Everything looks fine up here. I'm going to step outside and look around a bit. Are you okay?"

He had to strain to hear her answered "Yes."

He considered staying. There was no need for him to go out. There was no one close by. The town was a mile away, and there were plenty of people there, although if there had been a tornado and it had hit the town, they could use help digging out, and time would be of the essence, but he'd never heard the siren, so they probably hadn't been struck by a tornado.

But still, he needed to figure out what that crashing had been, first. Before he left to go help anyone else. And he wouldn't leave if Marlowe wasn't okay.

He reached the door and opened it, stepping out onto the porch which was still there. The ice-cream bucket that had skittered across earlier in the evening was gone, he noted, as he shone the flashlight back and forth on the wooden floor. But everything else looked just fine.

Even the sky had started to clear, and he could see stars as he stepped off the porch and down the steps. Still, something didn't feel right.

It just didn't quite feel the way it normally did. It took a minute for him to process, shifting and searching, before he realized the big oak tree that stood beside his house all of his life was no longer standing.

It was lying, not quite horizontal to the ground, but almost. Marlowe's house was holding it up.

The clouds shifted, and the moon came out.

Yeah. The tree had broken through the roof and looked like it had gone down through the second story, and possibly the cross members between the first and second story had caught it. The leaves weren't huge, but they were obscuring enough of his sight that he couldn't tell for sure.

One thing he definitely knew: Marlowe no longer had a house to live in. Not for a while anyway.

He could assess the damage better in the daylight, and he didn't stand and stare. He checked to see if their vehicles were there, and they were, both unscathed. He didn't see any other damage—just the tree on Marlowe's house.

His phone buzzed in his hand, and he looked down.

A message from his mother.

We're safe. Are you okay?

He answered quickly.

Yes, we're fine.

He asked about his brothers.

A few short texts later and his mother had reassured him that everyone in his family was fine and that the town of Cowboy Crossing had escaped unscathed.

His mother also said she heard from a friend that the next town over five miles away, Trumbull, had been hit by a tornado directly. But she wasn't entirely sure.

After telling her to let him know if they needed volunteers for anything, Clark turned and went back in the house. Somehow, he was going to need to tell Marlowe about her home.

She was strong, she'd weathered a lot of storms before, but it just seemed kind of unfair. To not have had a dad, then to have lost her mom and sister and now her home. He wasn't sure exactly how extensive the damage was, or whether they'd be able to get in to get anything out, but there was definitely going to be some major repairs necessary, and she wouldn't be in her home, probably for the summer, he would guess, especially since Trumbull had scored a direct hit and most cleanup efforts would be concentrated there, first.

Chapter 5

Marlowe had remained in the basement, clutching the kids to her and wishing that Clark hadn't had to go. She knew they needed to find out what damage had been done and whether or not they could even go back upstairs and go to bed for the night, but she hadn't wanted him to leave.

It wasn't even that she was scared, necessarily. She just hadn't wanted to lose...his presence, maybe? It had just felt like she was losing a part of herself when he walked away.

She tried to shake the feeling, because it was weird, and she was mostly successful.

It felt like she sat there forever after he said he was going outside to look around, but it was probably only a few minutes.

Funny how when Clark was with her, the time flew, and then while she was alone, it crawled.

Her throat was dry, and her stomach was tied in knots that she wasn't sure she'd ever be able to undo, but she was also extremely exhausted. Probably from the stress taking its toll. She just wanted to crash, but she didn't feel safe.

Then suddenly, light popped on outside the door, filling the cracks in the opening where the door hung on its hinges.

Relief made her laugh out loud, knowing that Clark had decided it was safe to check the light switches.

"Marlowe?" His form appeared in the doorway, looking black, as he was outlined by the harsh cellar light and her eyes were not used to anything but the solid blackness of the root cellar.

She wanted to struggle to her feet, but the two kids on her lap prevented that. She stroked their heads, smiling, because at that age, once they fell asleep, they could pretty much sleep through anything.

"Yes?"

He stepped further in. "I can carry the kids back up to their beds."

It was hard to define the exact signs that she picked up. Maybe because they'd known each other so long, but there was just something in the restless movements of Clark's feet or maybe the set of his shoulders or maybe even a tone in his voice that made her think that there was a problem. Although why she would think that, she had no idea, since he'd simply said he'd carry the kids up and put them to bed. He wouldn't be doing that if there was any danger.

"What is it?"

He snorted, an odd sound that contained no humor. "The house is fine. My house. Is fine."

Her eyes got big; if she had a free hand, she would have shoved it in her mouth to keep from saying anything, from squealing or crying as she wanted to. She had to swallow the sound, but she couldn't swallow her words. "What? Is my house gone? Was it a tornado? Is there anything left at all?"

"The oak tree. It's gone. Well, it's not gone exactly, it's just...lying comfortably on your house."

She sat in stunned silence, trying to process the implications.

"It's lying on the front part of your house. I can't tell exactly how bad the damage is, and of course, I'm not a builder or architect or anything close. I couldn't say for sure whether it was just a patch job, or whether it needs to be fixed entirely. I really don't know. My guess, if I were guessing, would be that it could be fixed. In the morning, we'll look at it, and I'll see if I can get in and get anything for you."

"No!" she said immediately. "There is absolutely no way I am allowing you to put yourself in any kind of danger."

"That's new," he said with a laugh.

"Oh, don't you even start joking with me now."

"How can I not call you out on that? Little Miss I-pushed-my-best-friend-into-the-deep-end-of-the-pool-when-I-knew-that-he-couldn't-swim-very-well. And I actually believe you shoved me out of that tree.

At least twice. Not to mention the time you tried to run me over with your car."

"Oh, stop. You know doggone well that I did not mean to run over you. Your foot is just bigger than I thought it was."

"Well, that's easy for you to say because you weren't the one that had a cast on your foot for six weeks because somebody broke five of your toes."

"That is a huge exaggeration. You had one broken toe. And the doctor said just take it easy. And gave you some pain pills. Which you loved, by the way."

"Yeah. They were some good stuff."

And just like that, she was laughing. Funny how he could do that to her. But she sobered, because losing her house was a serious matter. "This is one of the things the insurance will cover?"

She'd read the policy when she'd gotten it, and there were certain things, like an airplane crashing into her house from the sky, that the insurance wouldn't take care of. Being that they lived in Missouri, and tornadoes weren't exactly uncommon, she was pretty sure she remembered reading that it covered severe storms and tornadoes, although not floods, but in her distressed and distraught state, she couldn't remember.

"They cover tornadoes. We live in Missouri. I wouldn't have allowed you to get insurance that didn't cover tornadoes."

"Have you talked to anyone else? Is everyone okay?"

She thought of all the people in town, all of her friends and neighbors. The feed mill where she worked. Clark's family, who were almost like her family. "Your parents? Are your parents okay?"

"I talked to my mom. She said they, and all my brothers, and the town of Cowboy Crossing were fine. Some wind damage, like the tree out here. She did say she thought Trumbull had a touchdown, a direct hit possibly, but she didn't have any more information, and I thought it was more important that I take care of you and the kids. If she hasn't texted me back by the time we get them back in bed and you settled, I'll see if I can get a hold of Andy."

She was grateful he was going to call the fire chief and see if he could help, but thankfully he'd get the kids and her up first. "If you get Huck, I might be able to stand up with Kylie."

Their voices had been low and soft, and the kids hadn't even stirred. She wanted to get them to bed and get things settled, because as much as she'd like for Clark to stay with her, she knew he needed to get out and see if there was any way he could help anyone else.

"You just hang tight. I'll be back down in a minute." Clark's arms went around his son, and Huck groaned a little as Clark lifted him, cradling him against his chest.

Marlowe had always admired Clark with his son. It was funny that the goofball that she'd grown up with could be so tender and sweet. But there was no doubt about it; he'd been a great dad. She didn't want to wake Kylie, as much as for her sake as for Kylie's sake, as she didn't want to have to answer all the questions that were sure to ensue.

It didn't feel like any time at all had passed before Clark was back, carefully lifting Kylie and cradling her with the same gentleness he'd shown to his own child.

Something warm stirred in her chest. A little bit of a longing.

She supposed that was what other women termed their biological clocks. That longing to have a family.

She'd never really had that problem. Although occasionally, she thought about how nice it would be to have a husband to share child-raising duties with. Not very often though, because Clark was always there. She basically shared child-raising duties with him, and it had been working out just fine. She wasn't sure what was up with the sudden longing,

His lips were pressed tight as he moved slowly and carefully, trying to move her daughter without waking her. In the light from the cellar that shone in the door, her eyes hooked on those lips, and she remembered what she and her girlfriends had said about the high school Clark.

All of them had agreed that she was seven different kinds of lucky to have someone like Clark as her best friend. But they'd also all agreed that she was exactly that many kinds of unlucky, because with Clark having the most kissable lips in all of their high school, it was a pity they were off-limits to her, since he was her best friend.

What a weird time to think about kissing Clark. Although maybe that was the aftereffects of adrenaline. She'd heard about it but never experienced it herself.

"What?" Clark asked softly, pausing as he had been turning to take Kylie out of the room.

He'd caught her staring. Embarrassing.

"Nothing. I guess the adrenaline hasn't quite worn off. I'm a little shaky in getting back to normal."

"Yeah, me too. That's normal. As long as we know that's what's going on, the shakiness, and the weird feeling of things being a little bit surreal, and maybe even tiredness. Man, I don't know what all you're supposed to feel, but it's normal. It might even take a couple days to get it all out of your system. Don't be too hard on yourself." He chuckled. "I know, it's hard for you not to be hard on yourself. Just try."

He gave her a grin before he walked out of the room with Kylie.

If he only knew.

~~~

Marlowe stood at the kitchen window while dawn broke across the eastern sky. She hadn't slept well at all, of course, and she'd heard Clark walking around most of the night, too.

He'd actually left for a while, and she assumed he was going to help someone. He'd come back in an hour ago, just before daylight.

He might have sent her a text, but she hadn't checked her phone.

She breathed deeply through her nose as the brightening light showed the devastation that used to be her house.

Maybe she was being a little dramatic. The tree landed on her house and broke through. The front part was completely destroyed. But obviously, it wasn't a direct strike from any kind of tornado, and there would be plenty of things that would be salvageable in the back. If they were allowed in it.

"I was going to go over and get what I could out of there before people came and put the yellow tape around." Clark's voice came from behind her, and his hand landed on her shoulder. Again. She still hadn't gotten the feeling of that out of her head from last night.

Obviously, the adrenaline hadn't worn completely off yet.

"I don't want you to endanger yourself for us."

"I think you and I both know there's no danger. But it will be one of those things where they can't allow us to be in, because they'll be afraid we'll sue them if we get hurt in some way. It's almost light enough."

"Did you go somewhere last night?" She knew he had. And she assumed he probably knew that she knew. She just didn't ask the question that she meant. *Where were you?* That seemed...nosy somehow.

"I'd been keeping tabs on the Trumbull situation, from what I saw, no one died. But about two AM, they sent out a message asking for people to help take folks to a temporary shelter, and I figured I could do that much. I sent you a text."

"I haven't looked at my phone yet today." She knew her voice sounded fatalistic maybe. After all, she just lost her home. She didn't say that she just couldn't handle any more bad news, which was why she'd been avoiding her phone. "Where were the shelters you were taking them to?" She supposed she needed to think about that, because she would need shelter for herself and Kylie.

"Over in Sinking Springs. The Red Cross set up a temporary shelter in their rec building. I think it doubles as the municipal building, and it's in the back of the fire hall. There's lots of open space, and they had a bunch of cots set up when I was there."

She nodded, almost absently. "Did it look safe?"

His fingers tightened just a little on her shoulder, and he shifted behind her. "Safe? Yeah. I'd say it was safe. Not ideal, and definitely not private, but I think it'll be safe for everyone. That seemed like an odd question..." He seemed to be asking her where she was going with it, like he hadn't realized she'd need to be thinking about such a thing.

"I was concerned about Kylie and me. I guess that's where we'll be going."

"No." His voice was soft and gentle. Not a voice he used often on her.

They bantered back and forth more than anything, but she'd heard it a few times. Mostly when she got hurt. Although when she tried out for the school play sophomore year and hadn't made it and had been completely devastated, Clark downplayed the lead role that he'd landed and used that same voice to comfort her.

He'd used it again at her mother and sister's funeral.

"You're not going to a shelter. You're staying here. There are plenty of empty bedrooms, and Kylie is safe here. There's no way I would let you do that."

She turned to him, her arms crossed over her chest and her eyebrows up near her hairline. She wasn't even sure they stopped there. They might be going through the roof.

Then he would have a leaky roof too.

The thought almost made her smile. It would have if she hadn't been so annoyed.

"You're my best friend, and that gives you certain rights. I can't deny it. But you will not tell me what to do."

She set her jaw and turned back toward the window, but it didn't even take two seconds before she realized how stupid she sounded. He'd just offered her his home. A much safer place for Kylie than any shelter. And she wouldn't be taking up a spot that somebody else could be using.

Still, she let five more seconds tick by before she pulled both lips between her teeth and turned back, dropping her arms, shoving her hands into her pockets, and looking at the floor.

"I'm sorry. Thank you. Thank you so much for caring about us and for offering us your home. You know we'll take you up on it."

His hand had dropped from her shoulder, but now it came back up and grasped her upper arm. His other hand pushed up on her chin, gently and carefully.

"You forget who you're talking to, Marlowe. I know you like to be in control of your life. Complete control of everything. And last night, God showed you again that you're not. And you have a hard time with that."

He wasn't being arrogant, or she wouldn't be able to handle his words, would have to argue. But he was being sweet, like Clark often was and definitely could be.

"And yeah, I can see that I didn't make it any better by demanding that you stay here. I'm sorry. The idea of you and Kylie being there, and me not being able to protect you, gave me a sick feeling in my stomach. My words were definitely way more demanding than what you deserved." He tilted her head and chucked her chin. "I forgot who I was talking to. Nobody can tell you what to do, and anyone who tries is going to have you doing the exact opposite."

He was right about that. It was a character flaw she was working on. Everyone except for her mom and Elanor. She hadn't had a choice about Kylie when they died, and she hadn't even thought about not doing it. Kylie had become her world. She hadn't made a squawk of protest, nor did she want to.

"That's the most amazing thing about you, Clark." She tweaked his nose, just because he'd chucked her chin. She couldn't let him get away with it. "You aren't afraid to apologize. That's an appealing character trait in a man."

"It's my feminine side coming out."

"It's your smart side coming out."

"Well, before that smart side takes over, tell me what you want out of your house."

"I'm not telling you a thing. You better not be going in that house."

"Ha. I'm going in, and I'm going in right now. If you don't want me to bring you back the box of clothes you were going to donate to Goodwill, instead of the items that you most need, you better start talking, sister."

"I'm not qualified to be a nun."

"Don't I know it. That temper, holy cow. They'd have the abbey on lockdown before you even set foot off the bus."

"Are you done making fun of me?"

"Nope. The day's young, and I'm just getting started."

"This is a good strategy. You keep going on like this, and I'm gonna be like get your butt over to that house and get inside of it. Smart."

They laughed together. She knew there was no point trying to talk him out of going in the house, and she figured there probably wasn't any danger.

Much.

There was always some danger. Wasn't that life? Danger. Everyone worked so hard to avoid it. Not that one shouldn't. Just…sometimes a person had to take a risk. Physical risk. And…emotional risk as well.

She hadn't. Not for a long time.

"Oh no. Someone's gotten serious on me. You thinking them smart thoughts again?" he asked in his goofy voice that was always guaranteed to elicit a smile from her.

"Not really. Just wondering what combination of poisonous herbs the wicked stepmother used to get Snow White to sleep for a hundred years. I think I can slip that into your oatmeal later, and Kylie and I would have the house to ourselves."

"Yeah. That's what I thought. Deep stuff." He took a step toward the door. "You're gonna want the pictures off the walls. Your mom's jewelry box that's in the top drawer of your dresser, Kylie's baby books and the Bible on your nightstand that was your grandmothers."

Tears filled her eyes. She didn't care what weird things she'd been feeling. She walked over to him and put her arms around him, pressing her cheek against his chest, solid and familiar. "Thank you," she whispered.

His hands came up and slid down her back, bringing comfort. "Maybe I'll get Kylie some school clothes to wear today, too."

She laughed and swallowed against the lump in her throat. "Her hat for hat day."

"Of course."

His hands tightened.

"I guess the full effect of having my home damaged hasn't hit me yet."

"You're safe. Kylie's safe. That's all that matters in the end."

"You and Huck are safe, too. The tree could have fallen the other way."

"You're right. It could have."

"I can make more trips, but anything else right now?" he asked as she pulled away, straightening her spine and lifting her chin.

She gave him a list of a few more things, mostly stuff for Kylie, to help ease the transition, although Marlowe was pretty sure that Kylie would be fine. It would be a fun adventure to get to live with Clark and Huck for a while.

She decided to call in to the feed mill and tell them she wouldn't be in until at least lunchtime. That would give her a chance to call the insurance company and get their stuff settled in Clark's house.

She supposed she'd be moving into a bedroom too. She really didn't want to disrupt his life. Although, her moving into his house would be much less disruptive than him moving into hers. Just because of their personalities.

She was trying to do better.

She kinda thought he was too. They both knew that they were on opposite ends of an ideal center. Maybe that was another reason they got along so well, since they both knew they weren't perfect. It was always easier to get along with someone who could be shown their flaws, and admit that they have them, and who would be working on making them better.

Her heart still drooped, since she was not looking forward to the phone calls that she was going to have to make, but she was thankful that Kylie and she had been in Clark's basement last night and that he'd been concerned about taking care of her. She needed to remember to thank him when he came back.

Chapter 6

By the time Clark had made five or six trips from Marlowe's house to his, trying to get everything she had said she needed, she had the kids up, ready for school, and breakfast on the table.

"Are you sure they're having school today?" he asked, sniffing the air appreciatively. He wasn't used to someone cooking breakfast. Since his parents had built their dream home and moved out, breakfast had been on him. Sometimes, it hadn't been pretty.

"Yes, I checked online. Everything's business as usual."

"Okay, then I better get ready to go. They need to be there early today."

Her lips curved up as she continued to fork the bacon out of the skillet. He knew exactly why him remembering things made her smile. He wasn't the kind of person that one would expect to keep that stuff organized in his brain. He didn't expect it of himself, most of the time. But he put a lot of effort into remembering what he needed to for the children. His own life, not so much, but for the kids, it was worth it to make the effort.

He supposed he'd made that effort for his wife too. Maybe he hadn't been as good at it back then.

He sighed, annoyed at himself, because there was no point going back and reliving the past. Although he was sure there were a few things that, if he could do them differently, would make a difference. Now that he was older, he could see where he'd made mistakes.

At the time, it had been easy to blame her. Really, everyone else did, too. After all, she was the one who left. They were both immature, needing to grow up. It wasn't like he was the only one who made mistakes.

Maybe it wouldn't have made a difference after all.

But he could still be more responsible when it came to his son and any wife he might have in the future. And Marlowe, of course. Although he could still tease her.

"I called in to the feed store, and I'm going to be late today, while I make all the phone calls I need to about the house. Hopefully I can get them all done."

"Well, I just pieced together the planter yesterday in order to get the field finished, because I knew there was rain coming through, so I have some repair work to do, but if you need me to help you with any of that, you know I will."

She nodded, setting the plate of bacon down next to the one of eggs over easy.

Clark walked over to where Huck stood at the counter, a look of intense concentration on his face. "She put you to work, bub, buttering toast?"

"It was the only thing Kylie thought I could do without eating it while I was doing it."

"And he already licked the knife off twice. Which is really gross." Kylie's nose wrinkled up as she threw away the last of the eggshells, and she did look a little like she was going to be sick.

Clark suspected that part of Marlowe's new determination to not be so bossy and uptight stemmed from the fact that she could see a lot of herself in Kylie. Nothing like seeing someone else mimic you to see your flaws clearly.

"So I guess you're not having toast for your breakfast this morning, Kylie?"

"Mom said we probably already have the same germs since we spend so much time together. But if it were anybody else, there's no way I would eat after they licked the knife."

"But I like butter. It tastes good." Huck still looked a little confused, like he wasn't quite sure what exactly the problem was with licking the knife, even if he was in the middle of buttering toast.

"Huck, maybe you and I've been baching it for too long. We're about to be invaded. It doesn't feel good to be uncomfortable, but it might be good for us."

Their styles were so different – that's part of the reason they got on so well, because they complimented each other – it would definitely be an adjustment.

"Uncomfortable doesn't even begin to describe it. However, it will probably be good for all of us. Right, Kylie?" Marlowe gave her daughter a raised brow and a tilted head.

Kylie's lips pressed together, but she nodded slowly. "That's what you said earlier. I think it's one of those things I'm too little to understand right now." She smiled sweetly, if a little superiorly, to her mother.

Clark had to press his lips together and turn away from it. He wasn't going to laugh and encourage her little girl sassiness, mimicking words she'd probably heard a million times back at her mom, but she was also probably right.

They couldn't expect a five-year-old to understand how living with someone who is different than you were could actually make you a better person. Honestly, he wasn't even sure he understood that, although he could see the wisdom in it.

Marlowe let the comment slide, and she turned back to the stove to grab something. It was when she did that that his eyes caught on the curve of her waist, and he realized she'd changed her clothes.

She worked behind the counter at the feed store, so she never went to work dressed to the nines, like someone in the city might. But she had on a pair of khaki pants and a T-shirt that somehow showed her curves but wasn't tight, and he was sure the outfit probably wasn't intended to be sexy in any way or provocative. But somehow his eyes lingered and admired the graceful way her arms moved and her body turned. Remembering the rightness and the comfort of having her pressed to him last night, and also remembering the heat he'd felt that had been unexpected in so many ways but also felt exactly right, his eyes followed her as she sat down.

It wasn't until she repeated herself a second time that he heard what she said. He shook himself.

"Yes. Of course. I'll pray." He bowed his head and said a simple prayer, remembering to thank God for their safety and the safety of the people in their community, as he hadn't heard of a single life lost last night, although there had been plenty of people who'd ended up like Marlowe this morning, taking off work to call the insurance company and hoping to get a few valuables out of their home before it was condemned.

In his heart, he said a much longer prayer, because he was extremely grateful that Marlowe and Kylie had been with him in the cellar last night and that God had kept them safe along with Huck. The three people he cared about most in the world.

He picked the eggs up and helped both Kylie and Huck get one before he put two on his plate.

That last thought made him blink and sink deeper into contemplation. Did he really care more about Marlowe and Kylie than he did about his own brothers and parents?

He hadn't really consciously ever given it a thought before. Of course, he knew he cared about her. But more than his parents? His brothers?

Those thoughts were kind of uncomfortable, as uncomfortable as the idea that he had been staring at his best friend, and remembering the heat of their bodies being pressed together, and thinking that he might want to touch her again.

"Wonder how long it takes for the adrenaline of last night to wear off. You look that up?" He thought his question was casual. It had to be why he was thinking these weird things about his best friend.

He'd never been tempted to touch her, never thought of the heat between them as attraction, never had any ideas in his head like that at all. She was just kind of one of his siblings. Only now he wasn't having sibling thoughts about her. He didn't have any sisters, but he was absolutely sure that if he did have a sister, he wouldn't be staring at her across the table, admiring her, wanting to touch her again. That was just gross.

So yeah, definitely not sisterly thoughts.

"I'm sorry. I never did look that up. I do feel a little shaky this morning though. I'm not eating much because my stomach still feels a little odd. I don't have to go in to work until dinnertime, but I don't want to be sick and unable to talk on the phone."

He nodded. "That makes sense. What time does your ladies' gossip session start tonight?"

"You can have a little respect in your tone when you talk about the ladies of the town getting together to do good for the other residents of our community. Which is more than what was happening last night at your boys' gossip session."

"Hey, we get together and do good too. It's not easy to be a single dad raising a kid. We support each other. That's what a support group is."

"Hmmm." Marlowe didn't need to say anything more; she just raised her brows at him before she put a bite of egg and bacon in her mouth.

They grinned at each other over the table. They'd eaten plenty of meals together before, but this felt just a little different to him, and he wasn't sure exactly why.

Chapter 7

"There's some man and a blond chick that looks an awful lot like your ex standing on your front step. You might want to get yourself home and figure that out. She doesn't look very happy." Reid's voice crackled over the two-way as Clark lay under the planter, tightening a bolt.

His two-way was sitting on the toolbox. It was too far away for him to answer right away.

If he were a swearing man, he'd have some choice words to say under his breath. But typically, he wasn't, so he just took his frustration out on the bolt, yanking extra hard and stripping it out. Doggone it, it was the last one too.

He wasn't going to be able to get this planter fixed until he made it to the hardware store. Unless Marlowe would stop and bring one home. He pulled his phone off the clip on his side and shot her a text.

Her reply came back immediately.

Sure.

He knew he'd have what he needed by suppertime tonight.

That didn't solve his bigger, more pressing problem.

He'd forgotten all about his ex saying she was coming to visit.

Normally when she came, she stayed in a hotel, but because of the storm…he was betting they were full, which wouldn't have been a problem, except, if Dana was going to be in his home, he'd stay at Marlowe's house for a few days. Or with his brothers, one of them. Or his parents. Anyone.

But he could hardly bail on Marlowe the first day she'd moved in.

Rats. This was awful timing.

Sitting around and fussing about it wasn't going to help the situation. So he slid out from under the planter and straightened. Picking up the two-way, he pressed the button. "Thanks for the warning."

"Try to contain your happiness. I can't stand it." The voice sounded like Zane, but sometimes he had trouble distinguishing between Zane and Loyal. They sounded similar.

Regardless. Neither one of them would be happy if their ex showed up either. He had a good mind to say that, but he didn't. It seemed kind of petty.

"I got the planter done, except for one last bolt which I just stripped out. I'll come back over tonight and finish up. Might be dry enough tomorrow to get in that piece next to Hutchison Lane."

"Ha. Yeah, I wonder why you stripped that last bolt out. Probably didn't have anything at all to do with Dana showing up." That was Reid again, and Clark ignored him.

He loved his brothers, but none of them had seemed to have very good luck in the marriage department. He believed it seemed to be best for the males in their family to go solo.

Their mother might have had something to do with it. She was a perfect farmer's wife, and in his experience, he and his brothers had all picked out someone exactly opposite of her. He wasn't sure why.

Stupidity?

It didn't take long for him to wash his hands and jump in his truck. It wasn't that far to the farmhouse. Dana and the man—he assumed it was her new husband—were still there. What was the guy's name?

Clark tapped the steering wheel as he pulled in the driveway. Maybe it was Cody?

Dana would definitely be angry at him if he couldn't remember. Not that he'd ever met the dude. But if Dana mentioned it, even in passing, she expected him to remember it.

He was all about living up to expectations and all that rot, and when they were married, he had really tried to. But seriously, no one could be expected to remember every single thing that someone had ever told them.

Particularly the name of the man who took his place.

It wasn't really that he was still in love with Dana. It was just the idea that when he got married, he'd expected it to be forever. It was still a sore spot in his heart and life that it hadn't been.

And like most divorcees, her remarriage had been the final nail in that coffin. He couldn't deny that it had hurt. More than he expected.

But that was months ago, and he should be happy that Dana was here to see her son. Huck would be thrilled. It had been so long since he'd seen his mother last he'd even stopped asking about her.

"Where were you? We've been waiting outside! You knew I was coming today. I told you two weeks ago." Dana's perfect red lips were set in an angry, thin line, and her eyes were narrowed. Her hands sat on her narrow hips.

"Sorry." He forced the word out of his mouth. It was what she expected. He didn't want to be fighting when Marlowe showed up with Huck. Which would be anytime. "You could've gone in. The house is always unlocked."

"I know the house is always unlocked." Dana jutted one hip out. "I think you locked it on purpose today. Because it is most definitely locked, and I can't help but think that it was just some petty little thing that you did to make my life miserable. Isn't that a bit childish even for you? Can't we move beyond these little games that you play?"

She did that long blink thing with her eyes and a little sniff with her nose, the expression he always kind of thought made her look like a rhinoceros with allergies, but he assumed she thought it made her look like she was better than him.

Whatever.

"I did not lock the door on purpose. Maybe the handle's just stuck." He indicated the yard and the tree and the wreck that used to be Marlowe's house. "Things were a little crazy around here last night."

He didn't think his house actually shifted on its foundation. He hadn't felt anything like it, but he had no other idea why in the world the door wouldn't open.

And then it hit him. Marlowe would probably have locked it on her way out this morning. He refrained from rolling his eyes. Of all the days. But he knew that was exactly how Marlowe was. She probably didn't leave the house to go get the groceries out of her car without locking the door behind her. Not that there was anyone around to actually go into their house. She was careful that way.

It irritated him, but at the same time, he thought it was cute too.

Today, it bit him. Because Dana was already mad at him, and they'd barely spent sixty seconds in each other's presence.

As he walked up the walk, trying to remember what he had done with the spare key, he held his hand out. "Name's Clark. I take it you're Cody?"

"Yes." Cody held up his hand in a "stop" gesture. "I'm sorry, I didn't bring my mask today, because Dana assured me I wouldn't need it. But I'd prefer not to touch you. Germs, you know." He gave one of those fake face-crunching looks, where Clark figured he was supposed to assume the guy was sorry when, in reality, he really wasn't.

Clark didn't see the point, but he dropped his hand and nodded anyway. Relieved that at least he'd been right about the name. Hopefully they didn't ask him for the last one, because he really had no clue.

Unhooking his phone, he sent a quick text up to Marlowe.

Where is the house key?

Seriously? You don't know where your house key is?

Dana is here. Please.

Flower planter. Left side. Corner brick. Under that. Good luck. I'm just leaving the school. You want me to get lost on the way home?

He was already walking toward the brick, and he laughed out loud. Marlowe would have his back. She might lock his house up tighter than a maximum-security federal prison, or at least as tight as the lion cage at the zoo, which was more like what it felt like right now, with Dana on his property, but Marlowe would support him. Whatever he needed, she'd be there.

No. She's here to see Huck, I'm sure. You could probably stop and get him a soda on the way home. One with a lot of caffeine. Maybe she won't stay long.

He was being sarcastic, and he was pretty sure Marlowe would know that. She wouldn't give Huck caffeine or soda. Neither one was good for him, and Marlowe was all about healthy kids. Still. If it weren't for wanting to protect Huck at all costs, he'd be tempted to do it himself. Anything to get Dana to leave sooner rather than later.

He thought she said she was staying for three days. Maybe it was two. At the time, he hadn't worried about it, but with Marlowe here, and him unable to leave, it made a little bit more of a difference.

"I was going to stay at a hotel. But they're all full. Apparently, there was some kind of weather event here last night?" Dana put her nose in the air. "You guys make such a big deal about the weather, when there's so many more important social issues that we should be concerned about."

Dana was right there. They did do an awful lot of talking about the weather here. But their lives and jobs pretty much depended on it. While hers certainly didn't.

"Huck will be here soon. Marlowe's bringing him home from school."

"Well, I'm glad he's not here. Because I have something I need to talk to you about. Now that I am in a stable, married relationship, I've been thinking that I should have custody. Huck needs to go back to the city with me."

Clark froze. Key in hand, mouth open, his eyes shot to Dana. She was still as beautiful as she ever was. Flawless skin, those doe-brown eyes he could get lost in, and long curly brown hair that fell in waves around her youthfully slender body.

Maybe if she weren't so beautiful, he wouldn't have been blindsided. And stupid. He didn't really know what someone like her wanted from someone like him anyway.

His brain still hadn't fully processed what she'd said, and it took a lot longer than he wanted to admit before he got it to start processing again.

She wanted his child.

"But when you walked out, you gave up custody. We didn't even talk about it." It was the only thing he could think of to say. And he couldn't let her words hang in the air with no rebuttal.

"That's true. At the time, that was best. But now, we have space for him."

"Space? I have space for him. Having space isn't an issue."

She rolled her eyes. "You always make everything so difficult. You know exactly what I meant. Why do you have to jump on every single little thing and pick it to pieces?"

He stared at her. He never knew what to say when she started arguing like this. They'd been talking about Huck and his custody. And now all of a sudden, she was attacking him because he picked on her, which he hadn't done and didn't have anything to do with the argument at hand.

Why couldn't she stay on the subject?

But he knew better than to ask. Because it would degenerate into a real argument, with them both shouting at each other, and they wouldn't have anything worked out when Marlowe pulled in the drive with Huck.

He took a deep breath and blew it out. "I've provided a stable home for Huck since you left. Right where he was born, and I've done everything he's needed. I don't think Huck needs a different home. Although," he hastened to add, "I do think he enjoys visits from his mom. And I wish you could visit more often."

That was pretty much true. For Huck's sake, he wished Dana were here more often. For his own sake, he wouldn't mind if he didn't see her for another twenty years. Or longer. Whatever.

"You're such a product of your upbringing. Everything always needs to stay the same," she said in a singsong voice. "Nothing ever can change. We have to do things the same way our ancestors did them, and God forbid we have any kind of diversity or anyone ever introduces anything new." She rolled her eyes and gave him that look that said he was as dumb as a box of rocks. He really hated that look. "I want something different for my son. I want him to be educated. I want him to believe in science and not fairy tales. I want him to grow to become inclusive and not a homophobic jerk." She crossed her arms over her chest.

Clark waited for her to add the last two words, *like you*. He shoved his hands in his pockets.

Dana huffed. "Like you."

Yeah. Nothing changed. He'd argue with her, but there was no point. He could present all the facts and data he wanted to, but facts and data would never win an argument with someone who was only interested in calling him names.

The louder she said it, the more right she thought it made her. She'd always been able to outshout him.

"Are you going to unlock the door?" Cody asked. Honestly, Clark had forgotten he was there. "I have to use your facilities. It was a long trip, and I'd like to freshen up a bit. You do have an espresso machine, correct?"

"No, Cody. I'm sure there's no espresso machine or any other necessities that you or I might require. If those hotels had a single vacancy, I wouldn't even consider staying here." She lifted a slender shoulder and looked at Clark. "But we don't have a choice. When you're ready to be reasonable, I'm ready to discuss Huck's future with you."

Clark turned and went up the stairs, unlocking the door. He didn't want to hold Cody up from getting refreshed.

He held the screen door open as Cody walked in. Then he spoke to Dana as she went by. "I'm ready."

"You need to stop acting like a jerk, first of all. And secondly, you need to stop saying that I walked out on you, like that was some kind of character flaw on my part." She did the rhinoceros allergy thing again. "No one would blame me for leaving under the circumstances that I was living in. Not to mention, there's not a single person in the entire world who would think that I should've given up the opportunity that had fallen in my lap. And I couldn't do that with a small child. Plus, if I'd known how my figure would suffer with pregnancy and childbirth, I can guarantee you that wouldn't have happened, either."

Clark bit his lips in order not to say anything. He was pretty sure she hadn't said anything that was open for discussion yet.

"I don't think we need to go through a judge. As long as you can be reasonable. I'll take Huck back to New York with me. And you can come see him, as long as you give me a two-week notice. And not too often, because I don't want to have to spend all of my time entertaining you."

"As per our custody agreement, I was granted full custody. If you want to try to change that, you will have to contact the court, because I'm not giving it up. You're welcome to come see Huck any time you want to, and you don't have to give me any notice. But I'm not letting him go. And I'm pretty sure there's not a judge in the state who would say I should have to."

Actually, he wasn't sure about that. Even the judge in their case probably wouldn't have ruled that he got full custody over Dana, if Dana had wanted anything. But she hadn't. So there'd been no contention, and he'd gotten it all. All of Huck. He'd had to refinance his farm, because she'd got half of that.

"I should've known you wouldn't be reasonable about this. I came here thinking that we could actually talk like adults for once." Her eyes narrowed, and her lips pursed. "That's fine. If you want to fight about it, we can fight. Cody's father is a New York City lawyer. I'm pretty sure none of the attorneys you'll find in this hick state will be able to outmaneuver him."

She could be right about that. He lifted a brow and his shoulder ever so slightly, and she huffed one more time before walking by him into the house.

He hadn't seen nice Dana yet today. Probably the next time they talked, nice Dana would be out, and he'd wonder to himself why they couldn't have at least gotten along long enough to stay married and raise Huck. It was almost like she had a split personality. He never knew which Dana was going to show up on which day.

At times like this, with nasty Dana, he wondered what he'd ever seen in her and how he managed to get married to her. But she did have a good side. She could even be sweet, if not exactly funny. Volatile always, though. He'd kinda blamed himself, but he wondered if maybe it wasn't really him that set her off.

He was about to walk in after her when Marlowe pulled in. He could see her car kinda pause at her house, like she was going to pull in there out of habit. Then she gassed on it a little more, driving by her driveway and pulling into his.

He hoped she was holding up okay. A visit from Dana was probably about the last thing that she needed. But she'd always seemed to rub along okay with Dana, so hopefully they would this time too. Since Marlowe had her ladies' meeting tonight, she wouldn't have to put up with her.

His stomach recoiled at the thought. He didn't want to have to spend the evening alone with Dana and Cody. But it looked like that's what was going to happen. Along with Huck. Kylie would be there too. Having the children would be nice.

He walked to the car's passenger side as Marlowe brought it to a stop. Opening the door, he helped Kylie out.

"Whose car is that? Are there more people staying here too? Did someone else have a tree fall on their house?" Kylie looked at the odd car in their driveway, then up to him, her face part question, part assurance that he would know all the answers. He wished he did. All the answers to his own questions.

Like, was there some kind of curse in their family that made them incapable of picking out nice wives? Were he and his brothers destined to be divorced and alone? How could they all pick out bad women? It had to be them, right?

"No. It's Huck's mom." His eyes met Marlowe's over the top of her car before she opened the door for Huck.

"Yay! Mom's here? Did she move back in? Are you and Mom going to live together now? I'll have a real family, with my mom and dad really living together, like everyone else in my school."

Kylie had been climbing out, but she stopped and looked at the ground.

Clark supposed there wasn't too much in a kid's life that was worse than being different than everybody else. He couldn't fix it for Huck, and he couldn't fix it for Kylie either. Although right now, Kylie was sad, probably more because Huck had forgotten about her - she was the same as him - than she was about the fact that she didn't have a dad.

Clark was pretty sure she got sad about that at times, too.

"Hey." He touched Kylie's chin with one finger, lifting it up, so her big blue eyes met his. "As long as you're friends with Huck, you're going to have to remember men are notoriously forgetful and inconsiderate. You might as well just expect it."

Kylie's lips pressed together and curved down a little bit before she grinned a little-girl grin. Her head nodded. "I like him anyway. He's the best friend I have."

Huck had already jumped out of the car and had taken about two steps toward the house. But he wasn't so far away that he couldn't hear Kylie. He stopped and spun around and ran around the car, with a puppy-dog face only little boys could have. "I'm sorry. I forgot. You have a mom but no dad. I don't have a mom who lives with me. We're kinda the same. But," he tilted his head just a little, "we're the only ones. Right? Everybody else in our class has a mom and a dad?"

Kylie's brows drew together, and normally Clark would let them just have their conversation. But he kind of wanted to make a point. So he spoke.

"Huck, you might as well just figure it out now, no one else's life is as perfect as what they seem. Everybody has problems. They're just not your problems."

As he figured, Huck's face kinda scrunched up, like he was thinking about it. But most of Clark's words went over his head.

"Okay," he said, with as much unconcern as he'd said anything else. Happy unconcern. That was Huck. Clark didn't roll his eyes, but he kinda felt like it because that was probably men in general, at least most of the time.

"Mom's inside, right? Can I go see her?"

"Sure. She's waiting on you."

"I have a snack in the refrigerator for you two, and I'll get it out just as soon as you both go up and change your clothes." Marlowe had stopped on the walk where they were talking. "Kylie, I put your extra things that Uncle Clark brought from our house in Uncle Chandler's room where you slept last night. As long as we're here, that will be your room, unless," Marlowe's eyes went to his, "unless Uncle Clark needs us to move somewhere else."

Kylie had a big, happy grin, and her eyes shot to Clark's. He ruffled her hair and jerked his chin. "Go change your clothes. Everything's good."

Marlowe waited until the screen door shut behind Kylie.

"Is everything okay? Nothing has changed, has it?"

He didn't see any point in hiding anything from Marlowe. "She wants custody now and wants to take Huck to New York City and be a mom."

"Seriously? For five years, she's barely known he's alive, and now she wants to take him home with her? Just like that? Like tomorrow?" If possible, Marlowe seemed more upset about it than he was.

"If I asked that it would make me a homophobic racist, probably."

"Seriously? She's still calling you names? I thought she would have grown out of that by now."

"Yeah. I guess most of us learned in kindergarten stuff like that wasn't nice. But maybe that was some of my old-fashioned values coming out."

"No way. She was spouting off about that again too?" Marlowe's teeth gritted together as she huffed out a deep breath as though trying to control her temper. "You weren't kidding that nothing has changed."

"Yeah. Same old, same old, only now she wants Huck."

"You aren't going to let her have him, are you?"

"Did I tell you she got married?" Clark knew it wasn't exactly answering her question, but Marlowe wouldn't care. Not now anyway. He knew she'd be more concerned about him than herself over this anyway.

She gasped, and he assumed he hadn't. Probably a deliberate oversight on his part. Since he hadn't wanted to think about it.

"She did? Did you just find out?"

"No. It was a couple months ago."

"I'm your best friend, and you didn't think that was something you needed to tell me?"

"I never wanted to talk about it."

"Please don't tell me that you still love her." Marlowe's face lost some of her anger, and true distress took its place.

"I don't think so. I mean, no. No, I really don't."

"It sounds like you're trying to talk yourself into that. I mean, I won't think any less of you if you still love her. I'll question your sanity, maybe, but they do say love is blind. And in your case, if you still love Dana, it must be deaf and dumb as well."

Chapter 8

Marlowe almost slapped a hand over her mouth. She couldn't believe she'd said that.

"I'm sorry. That was rude. I know you still have feelings for her."

It wasn't hard to apologize, but it was harder than she thought to state that he still had feelings for Dana like it was okay. She had never been bothered by Clark's relationship with Dana before in her life. Why, all of a sudden, had she pulled into the drive, and seen Dana's car after getting the text that Clark had sent her, and felt like...smacking someone?

It was very much unlike her, and those feelings were definitely not welcome.

If this was still the adrenaline working through her body, she couldn't wait for it to leave.

Maybe she should drink more water.

Clark ran a hand through his short hair. "No, you're absolutely right. Why didn't you tell me how she was? Why did you let me marry her?"

"You never asked."

Clark dropped his hand, then he just kind of stared at her.

"Seriously? You couldn't have told me?"

"How do you think that would've gone over if I'd said, 'hey, Clark, I think Dana's a mistake?'" She spread her hands out in front of her. "You would've hated me, but you would've gotten over it. If Dana had found out? I would never have had a relationship with her. And that was the more important thing to me. I didn't want your girlfriend and eventual wife to hate me, because that would have meant I would never have seen you again."

Clark stared at her, his eyes opening and closing slowly. He probably didn't even realize it, but she could see the wheels in his head turning, rolling what she had said around, then testing it out. It was obvious he had never thought anything like that before.

"But if I'd asked? You'd have said something?"

She sighed and looked away for a minute. That was tricky. "Probably not. Not unless you'd asked me before you and Dana got together. I would probably have given you my honest opinion then. But once you guys were together?" She shrugged her shoulders with her hands out. "I couldn't say anything. I couldn't warn you. You wouldn't have appreciated it, and you know she'd have blocked me from your life."

He nodded, one lip pulled back.

Her chest felt woozy, like she was standing too close to the edge of a high cliff. And she wasn't sure exactly what that meant. It was almost like hope had blossomed there, but she was afraid to believe in it. But hope for what, she wasn't sure.

"How long until you have to leave for your ladies' aid meeting?"

Her brows went up. The very fact that he was using the correct name for her meeting showed that he wasn't himself.

"Gable?" She waited until he turned to look at her, stopping in the middle of the walk.

"Yeah?"

"Do you want me to stay?"

His eyes brightened before he looked away and shook his head, turning and continuing up the walk. She kept step beside him, but her mind raced. She didn't have to go. She was pretty sure he didn't want her to. Probably he didn't want to have to spend the evening with Dana and her husband, even with the kids between them.

"No. I don't want you to miss out on your meeting. I know you guys do good in the community, and with the tornado in Trumbull yesterday, I'm sure there are some things that you could be doing. They might even be thinking of helping *you*." They both glanced over at her house. Clark's tone changed, concern entering it. "How did that go today? Did you get everything done that you needed to?"

She nodded. "Pretty much. I think someone's going to be out over the weekend. Which surprised me. I didn't think I'd get anything accomplished until at least next week, since today is Friday. But they want to be on it, I think. Everything's going to work out."

"Good. I'm glad. I'm not trying to rush you out of my house. You know you're welcome to stay as long as you want, but did they give you a time frame?"

"I can stay as long as I want to?"

He paused with his hand on the doorknob, looking down and meeting her eyes. "Yeah. You can stay as long as you want to."

He wouldn't even joke with her, which bothered her.

"Now, Clark." She tried again, batting her eyes and slapping gently at his arm. "What would the neighbors think?"

His serious face broke into a grin, the first one of the evening so far. Score.

He looked around at all the open fields surrounding them and the road that cut through them. Theirs were the only houses in sight.

"I don't think the neighbors will care."

"You might be right about that." She knew he was. But she giggled. "I'm pretty sure the folks in town will have a heyday with what we're doing anyway. If my house gets fixed, and I stay here, that'll pretty much send them over the edge. We might get kicked out of the ladies' aid society and the single dad support group."

"I guess it won't matter."

That was a comment that was completely unlike Clark, and she put a hand on his arm, serious this time. "Why are you so down?"

"She's married. And she wants custody. She's got a New York lawyer. I don't stand a chance. The dad never does."

Her stomach flattened and deflated. She couldn't argue with that. She didn't know any single man who'd fought his wife for custody and won. The woman always won.

She didn't drop her hand from his arm. "I know you got it before, but it's because she didn't want him."

"Exactly. I have custody, and we work out her visitation on our own."

"I know. And you've always tried hard to accommodate her – not that she wanted to see him that often – so that she didn't get mad and try to go back and take it from you."

Clark's lips flattened and he nodded.

Why a judge considered a child to need his mother more than his father, Marlowe couldn't say for sure. She wasn't married and obviously didn't have a real family with Kylie, but Clark filled the role of a father, and it was very different from her role as the mother. They worked together, and they complemented each other. Neither one was more important than the other.

"Isn't there some way..." Her voice trailed off.

They stood there for about four seconds. Slow seconds that ticked by almost audibly, in slow motion. In that same slow motion, almost an out-of-body experience, their eyes drifted back to each other and kind of hooked there.

Maybe if they hadn't been best friends for her entire life, she would've had a problem trying to figure out what he was thinking.

As it was, she was pretty sure he knew exactly what popped into her brain at the exact same time it popped into his.

For some reason, she was very aware of her breath as it drew in slowly, flowed back out slowly, in slowly, back out slowly. Very aware of Clark's swirled brown eyes, darkening and changing, and his own slow breaths as they went in and out and in and out in slow-motion time with hers.

Maybe there was a breeze; there usually was. The scent of spring was all around them. Damp earth, fresh air. New growth and all that she loved coming to life in rural Missouri. She was aware of it all but wasn't thinking about it. Because the idea that had popped into her brain was so outrageous, so unthinkable, so perfect.

Absolutely perfect.

It would solve everyone's problems.

And Clark was thinking it, too.

Finally, his head shook ever so slightly, and his hand reached up to touch her arm, although it only brushed it before it dropped back down to his side like even that was now off-limits because of the awful thought that had entered their heads. "No. No. I couldn't ask that of you."

Another slow breath. And her lips parted. "You didn't ask."

His eyes seemed to search her face. "I didn't. Tonight?" His face scrunched up just a little, like he didn't understand something.

Her eyes dropped. And they landed on his lips. The lips that had been voted by her and her girlfriends as the most kissable lips in school. Those lips.

Nothing changed about that. She would still vote for those lips. The most kissable lips in town. The most kissable lips in Missouri. The most kissable lips she'd ever seen.

Stupid.

She dragged her eyes away.

Even as he shook his head more firmly. "No. We'll see how this shakes out. I don't know what kind of game Dana is playing, but I'm sure it's a game. She couldn't possibly want to take Huck with her. She didn't want that complication in her life before, and she hasn't changed that much. I'm just not sure what her angle is. But we don't have to do anything hasty. Or crazy."

His words made her throat tight. Of course. His lips were kissable, and she wanted him to touch her.

And he was doing everything he could to backpedal and get away from her. Of course.

She needed to back off. Way off.

Water. That's what she needed.

"I'm thirsty."

His eyes widened, surprised at her abrupt subject change. This was one of those things he wouldn't figure out. He would have no idea that she'd been secretly longing to kiss him practically all her life.

He shook his head, as if shoving the thoughts that had been running through it out of his consciousness. "Of course. You're just getting home from work. Let's go in. We'll figure out what we're having for their supper."

"Good. You're right. Supper first. And I'll help you however I can with Dana, of course." She sounded like she'd just run a mile or had a major surprise drop in her lap. But he didn't say anything, and she was thankful for his kindness in ignoring it.

He opened the door, and she walked in. Determined not to make a fool of herself over her best friend. Especially in front of his ex-wife.

Chapter 9

Clark walked inside still feeling a little dazed. He'd almost kissed his best friend.

No. That wasn't exactly true. He was pretty sure she'd had no idea that he'd had an overwhelming urge to close the distance between them, wrap his arms around her, and kiss her.

Pretty sure she didn't know.

He needed to make sure she didn't find out. That would totally ruin the best friendship he'd ever had. What he had with Marlowe rivaled anything that he had with his brothers even. And he loved his brothers more than he could say.

But what he had with Marlowe was special. A friendship that only came around once in a lifetime. He couldn't screw it up.

Not just for him. But for Huck, since he would be devastated if Marlowe walked out of their lives.

The idea that he'd had, that had floated into his brain, was as perfect as apple blossom petals on the spring breeze: that Marlowe and he get married.

It was the best and worst idea he'd ever had. The best for his heart. The worst for everything else.

Well, maybe marrying Dana was the worst idea he'd had. The worst mistake he'd ever made, anyway.

"Dana. Wow, it's been such a long time. And you look really great." Marlowe's voice sounded friendly and sweet as she walked around Dana who was sitting at a barstool at the island in the kitchen doing something on her phone. Neither Huck nor Cody were anywhere in sight.

Dana looked up and smiled. A real, genuine smile. "Marlowe. It's great to see you." She got up off her stood and came to give Marlowe a hug.

Marlowe walked toward her and Clark stayed out of the way, feeling like he needed to hold his breath so mean Dana didn't show back up.

Marlowe and Dana chatted like the friendly acquaintances they were while Marlowe walked around and grabbed the vegetable tray out of the refridgerator she must have prepared that morning, or even last night, for the kids to snack on.

Dana's eyes had gone back to her phone while they chatted, although she laughed at something Marlowe said. Clark inched toward the doorway. Maybe slip out and Marlowe could just handle things in here.

When Marlowe set the tray down on the counter, Dana's head popped up, her eyes narrowed, and her lips pursed.

Dana's eyes slid from Marlowe to Clark. Clark didn't have anything to hide; he met her gaze. The wheels were turning in her head, but he had absolutely no idea what she was thinking.

Dana tilted her head. "Are you and...Marlowe...living together?" Her eyes slid down to his ring finger on his left hand which had been bare since he'd taken their wedding ring off the day their divorce was final.

It'd been kind of foolish and pathetically romantic, maybe, on his part, that he kept it on until the paper was actually signed and recorded. Always having that hope that she'd change her mind and come back. He hadn't wanted to be the person whose marriage failed. He hadn't wanted to let Huck down.

"The wind blew a tree down on Marlowe's house last night. She's staying with me until it's repaired. That just makes sense." He hoped he sounded firm. Dana had a way of making him feel like an imbecile.

She lifted her brows like she didn't really believe him, then kind of shrugged.

"So how's life been in New York City? I heard a while ago that you were going to be a player off Broadway. How'd that go?"

Bless Marlowe for getting Dana to talk about herself. That was the one thing she seemed to be able to do without fighting with him. As long as they were saying good things about her.

They chatted for a while, with Dana mentioning her theater experience and what she was doing. Again, nice Dana seemed to be in the room.

The kids came out and grabbed some vegetables as Dana continued to talk about herself.

Clark didn't want to interrupt the conversation to ask about supper. He decided it was cowardly to leave Marlowe to have to deal with Dana by herself, so he grabbed a package of meat and put it in the microwave to defrost.

If Marlowe had something planned, she would probably say, but she didn't, so he just kept working on making spaghetti and meat sauce while Marlowe chatted with Dana.

"I'm not going to be here for supper," Marlowe said to Dana, as the conversation about Dana's theater career wound down, and Clark tilted an ear in her direction. "Clark has agreed to drive me in to my meeting. He had some errands in town he needed to run anyway. Is that still good with you, Clark?"

Earlier when he'd wanted to kiss Marlowe, it had been attraction. Plain and simple.

Now, he still wanted to kiss Marlowe, but out of attraction *and* gratitude. "Yeah, I have to get a bolt at the hardware store, plus I have a few other things I'd like to do in town. So yeah, I definitely am still in for taking you."

"Do you mind if Kylie rides along with you?"

"Absolutely not. I'd love to have her."

"Can I go too? Please? I like to go to the hardware store." Huck's eager eyes shifted from Marlowe to his dad.

Clark opened his mouth, but Dana beat him to it. "Darling, I want you to stay here with me. We have so much chatting we need to catch up on."

Well, Clark wasn't sure how that was going to go for her. Huck wasn't exactly the kind of kid that sat around and talked. He didn't have trouble talking. But he was usually doing something while he chatted. And he probably wasn't the slightest bit interested in chatting about Dana, which was the only thing Dana seemed interested in at the moment.

"Since your mom's here, son, you probably need to take advantage of spending some time with her." He didn't really want to say it, but he thought that was the right thing to do.

Dana pressed her lips together into a smug look. It was one he hated. So he looked away. His eyes landed on Marlowe, who was watching him. Her eyes were serious and gray like the morning mist and springtime. The kind of eyes she had kinda changed color, depending on what she wore and on her mood, too.

He liked them when they were that shade. Just a hint of green, a light green and pretty. With enough gray to make them mysterious.

"If you've got a handle on supper, I need to go take a shower."

Clark nodded. "Okay. I think Cody's in the bathroom at the end of the hall." He opened the microwave and flipped the meat. "Pretty sure your shower stuff is in a box on the floor of your room. That's where I set it. It was the last thing I brought over from your house this morning before I left. You can use my shower."

Marlowe nodded. The room he had was the only room that had a master bath. There was a powder room downstairs but not a shower.

"Thanks," Marlowe said, moving through the kitchen and out into the living room.

He watched her go. Familiar and yet new. Why was he noticing her all of the sudden? Did one hour in a storm cellar with their bodies pressed together change the way he'd thought his whole life?

Sure felt like it.

If it weren't for risking their friendship, and Huck's security, he really thought he might go after her. She was definitely the kind of girl he wanted. After his disastrous marriage with Dana—not doing that again. He wanted someone exactly like Marlowe.

He finished making spaghetti and had the kids sitting at the table with plates in front of them—Cody and Dana had kind of politely declined—before Marlowe came back downstairs, dressed in a flowing skirt and a fitted T-shirt. He hadn't seen that outfit in a long time.

"Can't find any of your usual things?" he asked with a grin.

He had to admit he'd been in kind of a hurry this morning when he'd been grabbing her stuff and throwing them into a bag.

"Exactly. That, and some of the things I'd normally wear are kind of wrinkled. I'll have to spend some time sorting things out. I'm not complaining though, honestly, I just really appreciate you going over and getting them."

Sometime during the hour or so that they had been home, someone had stopped at her house and put yellow caution tape around it. Clark noticed that as they walked down the walk.

"I really appreciate you saying that. But I especially appreciate you getting me out of spending the evening stuck in the house with them tonight. As much as I hate to leave Huck."

"Good. I kinda hoped you felt that way. I would have felt really bad if you wanted to be there."

"Yeah. I wanted to be anywhere but in the house with my ex and her new husband."

"Are you sure you're okay with that? You seem a little upset."

"No. Not really. I guess it just feels like another kick. You know? Like, she left me, and that was a kick. She served me divorce papers, and that was a kick. She didn't want our son, that was a really hard kick. A new boyfriend every few months, and each time, that was a kick. Not really because I was jealous or anything, just because it was just one more kick. Each time, she's saying, 'you're not good enough.'"

Someone had diarrhea of the mouth today. He didn't usually get that sappy and emotional about his divorce.

But Marlowe had asked, and they'd never really talked about it.

He wasn't in love with Dana. He didn't even really like her. But she could hurt him. Because they had been married. Everything she did, everything that had to do with him and his child and his ex-wife finding someone else to love, just said loud and clear, *you weren't good enough.*

"I guess there aren't too many people that are good enough for Dana. According to her anyway." Marlowe cast a concerned glance in his direction, and he met her eyes and shrugged.

"I guess her getting married would have to be the last kick, right? There can't be anything else."

Marlowe's lips pressed tight together; she looked away.

He stopped with his hand on his truck door latch. "I'm asking you. Tell me, what could make this worse? You're saying this couldn't be the last kick?"

Her eyes got a little wider; she breathed in.

Kylie had been sitting on the porch steps, playing a video game with earbuds in, not noticing them at the truck. Marlowe called her and Kylie started toward them, walking slowly, still playing.

Marlowe waited for her to get in the back and buckle herself. Then she opened her own pickup door and got in.

Clark followed her, slamming his door shut behind him, putting his hand on the key, but not turning it. Waiting.

"I think you could go on," Marlowe said in a soft voice, making sure Kylie was still concentrating on her game. "If she gets custody. If she takes Huck away. If Cody and she have children together." There was a small silence. "I don't know. I've never been through it. Those are just a few of the things I can think of."

He felt like slapping the steering wheel, and for the second time that day, he kinda wished he could swear and get away with it.

"Thanks."

"You asked. I wouldn't have told you otherwise. Especially since you'd just asked today why I didn't tell you about Dana. So I could hardly not tell you about this, since you specifically asked me outright."

He started the truck back down the driveway, pulling out onto the road and heading toward town without saying anything.

After a few minutes of silence, Marlowe spoke again. "I know you're not happy about this, and that's what your silence means. But it feels like you're angry at me. And I wish I hadn't said anything."

"I'm sorry." He blew out a breath. "I'm definitely not angry at you. And you're right. I hadn't thought of those things, and I'm not looking forward to them. But thank you for saying something. I'd rather be prepared. I guess. Although, I suppose I'd rather just not think about it at all."

"Well, that's pretty hard with Dana here. But she usually doesn't stay long. She usually doesn't visit at all, actually. Will she be here until tomorrow?"

He loved the little hopeful note in her voice. "Someone else is looking forward to them leaving?"

"Of course. Your best friend. I hate it whenever she comes around, because you get gloomy and morose and depressed and I start to worry about you."

She said that last part a little softer and a little fast, like she almost didn't want to admit it. So of course, he had to jump on that.

"You worry about me? Worry? Really? So like how worried is worried?"

"You keep talking like that, and I'll not only stop worrying, but I will find a way to leave you alone with Dana for the rest of her stay."

"Fine. Worry about me. I don't care."

Chapter 10

When Marlowe walked into the church basement, she was greeted by the smell of coffee, mixed with cinnamon and brown sugar. Lynette, the pastor's wife, must have made her famous cinnamon rolls. For some reason, Marlowe felt like she could really use some.

She made a mental note that if there were any left over, she'd take some home for Clark. She didn't consider that emotional eating, as much as she knew it would cheer him up a little.

Having his ex around was always hard just because of the nature of their relationship and how it ended. And maybe even because she hadn't wanted their son. When Clark said it was like a kick, he wasn't joking.

She'd seen it.

"Marlowe!" Lynette said in her soothing, sweet voice. She and her husband had eight children; she homeschooled them and handled all the many and varied duties of a pastor's wife with enviable competence. Lynette had been born to be a pastor's wife. Although the town had had a little trouble accepting them at first, because Deacon Hudson, Clark's brother, had been expecting to take over the church when the old pastor retired.

Marlowe didn't think the circumstances that surrounded his inability to become ordained should have affected whether or not he was given the pastorate here, but it had.

Despite the unfairness and the pain, Deacon had handled the situation with as much class as anyone could. Marlowe just hoped someday the truth came out. She couldn't hold all that against Lynette though. Lynette was doing the very best she could, and Marlowe loved her.

"Your cinnamon rolls smell amazing. I didn't even know I was hungry until I walked in."

"Well, you can have as many as you want, because I made a triple batch."

"Fantastic. If there are any left, Clark would love to have one."

"I heard his ex was in town. I made some for the tornado victims, and I set two back for him and one for each of your kids." Lynette's face looked serene and joyful. There could be no doubt she loved her "job" as pastor's wife.

"Thank you."

Before Marlowe could say anything else, Lynette spoke again. "We've organized an auction to benefit the families who lost their homes, businesses, or other personal property in the town of Trumbull. Maybe you've heard about it."

Lynette held out a piece of paper with the word "auction" in big block letters at the top.

While Marlowe was skimming over it, Lynette spoke again. "Clark's brother, Chandler, agreed today to donate *one month* of his time to be sold at auction." Her eyes were bright with excitement. "We've done dinner or a day before, but this is huge, and I'm expecting it to bring in a lot of money! Just the magnitude will draw people to the auction so some of the lesser items will make money. I'm not sure..." Her voice trailed off. She tapped her chin with her finger. "My husband was not sure that this was a good idea and of course will make sure that nothing lascivious will be going on. He's offering his companionship or work. Nothing of any sinful nature."

"Of course," Marlowe said. A few years ago, she would have said Chandler would never have agreed to that anyway. But every time he came back from Hollywood, he seemed a little more jaded. It wouldn't shock her to hear that he lost his small-town values. As much as it would disappoint her and his family.

But she didn't say any of that. It would just be gossip.

"Thanks for sharing this. If you don't have one already up in the feed store, I can take it to work on Monday and put it up."

"Oh, if you would, that would be fabulous." Lynette reached over and grabbed the clipboard that was sitting on the table beside the flyers.

She skimmed down through the list and struck a line through feed store.

The door opened, and Clark's mother, Emma, walked in. Lynette called a greeting, but Marlowe walked over and hugged her.

"I was worried about you last night. I'm glad to see you're safe."

Emma, as beautiful as she'd always been, patted Marlowe on the back. "As I was worried about you. But Clark texted me, and I knew he was looking after you. I was sure you'd be fine."

Emma had been like a surrogate mother growing up. After all, Marlowe's mother was a single mom and worked a lot. With Clark and her being so close, Marlowe had spent a lot of time at their house. Then, after the car accident, Emma had truly stepped up. Only Clark had supported her more.

It was really hard to imagine, looking at Emma, that she had raised five boys.

It wasn't hard to imagine, however, that Emma was the mother of one of the hottest stars in Hollywood.

"Clark said you were taken care of, so I haven't been around. Trumbull has so much damage, and I've been collecting blankets for the folks who've been set up at the rec building." She put her hand on Marlowe's arm and looked deep into her eyes. "Are you really okay?"

"I'm fine."

"And Kylie?" Emma loved her like a grandchild.

"She's perfect. It's like an adventure to her."

"I figured." Emma leaned back, and her stance became casual again. "Did you hear that Chandler has donated one whole month of his time to the highest bidder at the auction that Lynette has organized?"

"Yes. Lynette just told me about it." Marlowe looked over to her. Lynette was talking to Melody, Cowboy Crossing's only dog groomer.

"Oh, I know what I wanted to ask you." Emma turned her full attention to Marlowe. "I heard from Sam down at the grocery store who told him that Sally, Ray's wife, had heard from Quinton that Dana was in town. Is that true?"

"Dana is in town," Marlowe confirmed. She understood why it was so hard to believe—Dana hardly ever visited.

"How? I mean, the hotels are full. Did she have a reservation?"

"Dana is staying at Clark's house." Marlowe tried to say that without inflection.

But Emma understood immediately how that would affect Clark. She tapped her toe. "I should offer to have her stay at my house. Only... No, probably not. My maid was one of those whose houses were damaged. She's brought her whole family and a sister and her family to my home. If I'd known earlier..."

"No. I'm sure Clark will survive. Your maid and her sister need a place to stay."

Emma looked like she was going to say more, but several more people had gathered, and Lynette called everyone over to the table. They'd all moseyed over when the door opened one last time.

A hesitant head poked around the door before the body followed.

Marlowe heard several gasps, and the room, which had been buzzing with noise, fell silent.

Ivory, who some people called out of the side of their mouth the town's drunk in the feminine form, took a hesitant step inside. Then another. She closed the door behind her.

This was the first time Marlowe had seen her in the church at all. Once in a while, she saw her around town, always wearing a long trench coat and a scarf and a slouch hat. She came into the feed store some, but she usually ordered her feed to be delivered. If she got any.

She always paid her bill on time.

They weren't at the feed store, and it might not be part of her job right now, but it was part of being a Christian, so she walked across the quiet church basement as the other ladies in the group stared.

All except for Lynette. As Lynette walked, she stretched her arms out and made a beeline for Ivory, obviously intending to hug her, trench coat and all.

"Oh, Ivory! I'm so glad you could make it. I was really hoping you could come." Lynette threw her arms around Ivory, and Marlowe slowed to a stop, feeling a little unneeded, because Lynette was a welcoming committee of one. "I'm so glad you're here, I've been giving everyone copies of my auction information. It's hot off the press."

She wiggled the paper in her hand, and Ivory looked at it for a few seconds before hesitantly reaching up and taking it from her.

Her hands looked dirty, but Marlowe had been around working men long enough to see that what looked like dirt was probably just grease that had not washed off when she'd washed her hands. It took a stronger soap than most people kept in their kitchens to get that kind of grease off hands. Ivory either didn't know about it, didn't have any, or didn't use it.

It didn't matter. Not to her. She closed the distance between Ivory and herself and decided it didn't really matter she'd never spoken to Ivory before in her life; she could hug her too. So she threw her arms around Ivory and said honestly, "I've always wanted to meet you. I've seen you in the feed store and waited on you once or twice. But I'd like to chat. I'm so glad you've come."

Ivory nodded. A couple of strands of hair that were so blond they almost looked white waved in the breeze beside her head.

"And that amazing scent that you're smelling right now is Lynette's fantastic cinnamon rolls. I'm pretty sure that when God says manna, he means Lynette's cinnamon rolls."

Lynette's laugh filled the air. "Oh, you're too sweet. They're not that good. But people do seem to like them. Come on over here and sit down. We're going to work on things that we can do for the auction to make money for the tornado victims. I'm sure you have lots of good ideas, and I'll introduce you to any of the ladies that you've never met."

Marlowe trailed along behind as Lynette put her arm around Ivory's shoulders and guided her to the table where the other ladies looked at her as though Lynette were bringing over a live bee nest.

Marlowe waited until Ivory had sat down, Lynette on one side, and Marlowe took the other side. None of the ladies there meant to be rude; they were probably just really surprised, and it was certainly understandable to be distrustful of someone that they didn't normally talk to.

Marlowe suspected Ivory was shy.

Sometimes, shy people were labeled odd.

It also might have something to do with the fact that Ivory was the daughter of the town prostitute, who was now retired. Although she did not attend church, she was considered loosely reformed. Enough to stay out of jail, anyway. Rumor also had it that Ivory's father was the ex-town drunk. He had died under the park bench several years ago. Homeless.

But Ivory's mother laughed at that, because she said she really had no idea who Ivory's father was.

The evening wore on, and Marlowe was impressed, yet again, with Lynette's organization and planning. It was amazing that Lynette was able to homeschool their eight children and still do all the things that she did. She had no idea what her husband would do if anything ever happened to Lynette.

By ten o'clock, Clark had texted her.

I'm outside. How much longer is this going to last?

The meeting was still going strong, but they had pretty much organized the auction, and Marlowe had volunteered for several jobs. She didn't need to stay.

I'm coming out. Give me three minutes.

She said her goodbyes and whispered in Lynette's ear about the cinnamon rolls, and Lynette told her where they were.

She got them and slipped out the back door. Clark was parked right beside it, and his truck started as soon as he saw her.

"How'd it go?" Clark asked as she climbed in.

"It went pretty darn good. I scored two cinnamon rolls for you, one for Huck, and one for Kylie." She turned around, looking to smile at Kylie in the back seat, but Kylie was sound asleep.

"She must have been pretty tired." Marlowe kept her voice down and smiled at her sleeping daughter. Such sweet innocence. Man, she hoped she could do a good job of raising her.

"Yeah, I went to Reid's house, and she was out running around with his twins, chasing the goats, and trying to ride their dog."

"Oh, poor dog. Did he survive?"

"Everyone was alive when I left. But Kylie didn't stay awake for more than a mile or two."

"How's Reid doing? Did he survive the storms okay? Did you tell him about our house?"

"Oh, he already knew about it. Come on. It's a small town. Soon as the light dawned on it this morning, the first car that went by stopped at the convenience store and told Mabel. By the time we'd sat down for breakfast, the whole town knew."

"Okay. You're right. I have to admit I wasn't thinking."

"Well, that's not the first, but it is pretty unusual."

"I think you just complimented me."

"It was a slip. Sorry."

She snorted. "And here I was going to give you your cinnamon roll. But never mind. I'll probably want to eat it myself in the morning."

"I'll tell Miss Lynette you didn't share."

"Miss Lynette will totally understand why I didn't share. Trust me, she's a woman, she's on my side."

"No. All I have to do is tell her I'll take her older boys for the summer, and she'll be on my side." His dimple flashed as he put the pickup in gear and pulled away from the church. "She'd love to see her boys working on the farm."

"You're probably right about that. Here." Marlowe held out the cinnamon roll.

Clark looked both ways before he pulled onto the highway, then he grabbed the roll from her.

They'd handed things to each other a million times before. All their lives. But this time when their fingers brushed, it was like there was a small explosion in the cab of the truck. At least for Marlowe.

Thankful it was dark, she snapped her hand away so quickly Clark almost dropped the cinnamon roll. That was awkward. She felt like she needed to apologize. But that would only bring attention to the fact that she'd acted weirdly, for absolutely zero reason, except all of a sudden she felt sparks and explosions when she touched her best friend.

She said the first thing that came to her head. "What do you think the chances are that Dana and Cody will be in bed when we get home?"

"Hopefully a hundred percent," Clark answered, and she believed that was truly what he wanted, but his voice lacked its normal humor.

She wasn't sure if it was because of her odd behavior or because of him still carrying a torch for his ex, even though he claimed he didn't. It still upset him somehow to talk about her, and Marlowe couldn't help but believe it was because there was still something there for him. As much as he denied it.

"Oh, Jill texted me, and she wanted to have the kids next weekend. Both of them. I told her I thought that was okay."

Jill was Dana and Alonzo's mother. Which made her the grandmother of Huck and step-grandmother to Kylie, since Alonzo wasn't Kylie's biological father. Elanor had never told Marlowe all the details, but she'd been pregnant with Kylie when she'd married Alonzo, who'd known the baby wasn't his, yet loved Elanor and married her anyway.

Jill lived about fifty miles north of them and didn't see the kids much, but normally took them both for a weekend every few months.

"Yes, that's fine. It will probably work out for the best too, since maybe they'll be working on my house by then."

"Maybe. I think I heard somewhere they were putting priority on houses, versus garages and other outbuildings. Which makes sense."

"Yes. It does. But as long as I'm not being too much of a pain for you, I'd like to see the people who are in shelters be taken care of first." She clasped her hands together in her lap. She hadn't realized until then how much she was enjoying being even closer to Clark. Being with him was comfortable, yet exciting at the same time, especially with the new feelings that she'd been dealing with since the tornado.

"Of course. And you're not the slightest bit of a pain. You cooked breakfast."

"Well, I know it hasn't been easy for you since Dana's there too."

"It's all Dana. Nothing to do with you."

She believed that. He was probably just being honest.

She tried to look on the bright side. "Now we have something to look forward to. Not only should Dana be gone by next weekend, but the kids are going to get to spend a fun weekend with Jill. They always love it at her house."

"Yeah. That's nice. Jill and Dana couldn't be any more different from each other. It definitely eases my mind to let Huck go, when I know that he's gonna enjoy himself."

"Exactly."

Marlowe ran a finger down the seam of her skirt, searching for a topic that would be neutral. She still felt a little off-kilter with Clark, and the conversation just felt a little stilted.

"Have you figured out why Dana wants Huck?"

"No. But I have a feeling it has something to do with money or possibly a part she wants to play. I suppose it's cynical of me to say, but I can't see where she's changed at all."

"I suppose someone might call that cynical. I call it reality."

He chuckled. "Thanks."

Chapter 11

Thankfully, Dana left Monday morning.

Unfortunately, she wanted to come back the next weekend. When Clark explained to her that Jill was taking Huck for that weekend, she threw a bit of a fit.

"I think you set that up just so that I wouldn't get to see him next weekend." Her eyes were narrowed, and she glared at him across the counter.

He hated always feeling like he was on the defensive, and for goodness' sake, it was her mother. Dana didn't get along with Jill, though. "How was I supposed to know that you were thinking about coming back next weekend to see him?" He gritted his jaw and tried to pull a deep breath in and blow it out before he said any more. "You haven't seen him in over a year. And now all of a sudden, I was somehow supposed to know you want to come and visit two weekends in a row? If you would tell me, I would make sure that he was here. But Jill had already set up to have them."

"You're so unreasonable. It is impossible to talk to you. The fact of the matter is I am his mother, and I should take precedence over anyone else. Cancel my mother's plans, and have him here next weekend."

"It's your mother. Go to her house and see him." Clark didn't really want to suggest that. He wasn't completely comfortable with the thought of Dana seeing them at Jill's house. Dana was just the kind of person who would put Huck in the car and disappear with him.

Eventually the law would come after her and find her, but Clark didn't want to put Huck through that. Man, he wished he hadn't screwed up so bad for his son. Why hadn't he been smarter when he'd been thinking about marriage?

"Well, I just might do that."

Clark turned to the refrigerator and opened the door, not even remembering what he wanted to begin with. Just frustrated. He didn't really think Dana would go. The two of them didn't get along very well. What a mess.

It wasn't long after that Dana drove away, giving up on getting Huck, and leaving Clark with a profound sense of relief.

The rest of the week went well for him. They were ahead on the corn planting by Friday, and he and Marlowe had settled into a routine. The only hiccup being Tuesday evening when Marlowe went to use the washing machine and had to move his clothes from the washer to the dryer.

"You put your socks and your jeans in the same load of clothes, along with Huck's white T-shirt and his red sweatshirt. Who does that?"

She'd waited to say anything until after they put the kids in bed at least. Neither one of them had mentioned the idea of them getting married. He hadn't allowed his brain to go there, and he assumed she hadn't either. Although he was completely certain that if it were something that was necessary for him to do to keep custody of Huck, Marlowe would do it in a heartbeat. He just didn't want to take advantage of her in that way.

He had a feeling he'd do it for Huck, if it came right down to it, though.

"I don't understand what the problem is. All the clothes got clean, right?" He stood with one hand holding onto his neck and one hand gripping the basket that he'd been about to set on the counter by the washer.

"It's not about getting them clean as much as it's about having them fade and run into each other."

"They kind of have to run into each other in the washer, don't they?" He managed to keep his lips from twitching.

"You're not even funny. The colors run, and then you don't have white socks anymore, you have gray or pink because of the red sweatshirt, and everything just gets yucky. Didn't you ever learn how to wash clothes?"

"I sure did. Right here's a clean load. Washing clothes is supposed to get them clean. You want to get all picky about it, go right ahead, but you're just making more work for yourself."

She sighed and shook her head and grabbed her ears like she wanted to pull them off.

"That's new."

"What?" Her head snapped up, and she looked around.

"You grabbing your ears. I've never seen you do that before."

"That's because I've never been quite this frustrated before." They both knew that was a major exaggeration. For the most part. "How can you think that's okay?"

"I'm not dropping an atomic bomb on anybody. I'm not sending anyone to hell. This is not a moral dilemma. This is a personal preference. I prefer ease of laundry over...whatever." He waved his arm in the air, searching for a word. What English word was there that meant someone was making way more work for themselves than they needed to? "You're making a mountain out of a molehill. There. It's ridiculous. You can have the laundry done in one load, or you can do three loads and have it take all day. To me, that's a no-brainer."

"No-brainer. That seems fairly accurate." She had one arm crossed over her stomach, and the other tapped her chin.

It was a typical Marlowe look, and he kind of forgot about their argument as he watched her finger touching her chin. Then his eyes slid to her cheeks which were bright pink, indicating that she was upset.

Which he found funny. Upset over laundry. Ridiculous. Especially upset over clean laundry. Seriously? And even after working all day, with her hair in a ponytail, and wearing an old T-shirt and loose jeans, she looked good. Her bare feet poked out of the jeans. Her nails were painted some kind of purple-red color. That color didn't really go with Marlowe's personality, but it looked kind of cute.

"You're not even paying attention."

His head snapped up, and he realized he must have missed at least a line or two of what she'd said. He didn't usually have trouble keeping his eyes from looking at her. And he couldn't even blame this on adrenaline. That storm was almost a week ago.

"I'm sorry. You're right. I wasn't paying attention. What color of nail polish is that anyway? Looks like something a teenage girl would wear."

"Did you just call me old?" Now both hands were planted on her hips, and her anger was only partially feigned.

Uh-oh. This was not easy, funny Marlowe. He didn't like to be on the receiving end of Marlowe's anger.

"I was kidding. Totally kidding. That looks like the perfect nail color for a woman of your years."

"Did you mean to say advanced years? Because I think you paused right there between 'your' and 'years.'" She took a step toward him. Menacing.

Okay, yeah, he didn't like it when Marlowe was angry at him, but there was some kind of new jolt thing happening in his stomach, and his heart was doing something weird as well.

He shook his head. He needed to get his thoughts straightened out before he screwed everything up for good.

But his feet hadn't gotten the memo that his brain just sent out, and he moved one step closer to her. "There's nothing wrong with your age. It's the same as mine. And I kinda like it."

That took the wind out of her sails, and she deflated almost visibly before his eyes.

She shook her head. "I don't know why that upset me so much. You're right. You are the same age as me. I guess I'm just completely shocked to see that someone in the industrialized world would do laundry like this. It's just unimaginable. I never suspected that you were a closet...I don't even know what to call it. Crazy. No one does laundry like that."

"I bet all of my brothers do laundry like that. I can't imagine any one of them takes the time to separate socks and underwear from jeans and shirts, and what did you say about you can't wash red or something? Who ever heard of that?"

"You're kidding, right?" Her tongue came out and touched her lip.

He shook his head, losing his train of thought as he kinda watched what she was doing. Only for a couple seconds. Then he turned abruptly away. "I'm gonna take these upstairs and put them away."

He walked away. Man, he had to stop acting stupid around Marlowe. He couldn't even concentrate on an argument he'd obviously been winning.

"I said I was sorry. I really am. I didn't mean to insult the way you do laundry. You can do whatever you want with your clothes. I'll just start washing Huck's things, okay?"

He reached the stairs and started up, answering without looking back. "Sure. You can wash anybody's clothes you want to."

"As long as I can do it my way."

"Sure. Do it your way."

~~~

"Have a great afternoon," Marlowe said to Mr. Bovary as he nodded at her, then picked up his bag of cat food and a packet of sweet corn seeds and walked out of the store.

She looked at the customers that just came in. Mr. and Mrs. Cromwell and their four children browsed the aisles.

Their children, all too young for school, were always well behaved, although Mr. Cromwell was sometimes so unkind to his wife sometimes that Marlowe just wanted to grab a hold of him.

She wasn't normally a violent person. But Mrs. Cromwell was about the nicest person ever. She completely exemplified dignity, grace, and the Bible teaching of meekness. Or maybe deference. Whatever it was, Marlowe admired her almost as much as she pitied her.

She glanced at her watch. The kids were getting out of school early today, and Clark had agreed to pick them up since they were ahead on the corn planting.

Jill was scheduled to arrive at the feed store anytime, since she was going to meet them there so Marlowe could say goodbye to them before they left for the weekend. She wouldn't see either Huck or Kylie until late Sunday night.

"Go out to the car and get my wallet." Mr. Cromwell's voice carried down the aisle. He didn't sound particularly nice, and he definitely didn't say please. But Mrs. Cromwell smiled graciously, and with the baby in her arms, and holding onto the hand of their second youngest, she started toward the door.

Mr. Cromwell had his cart next to the dog food aisle, and he was putting a fifty-pound sack in it.

Mr. Long, the manager of the feed store, met Marlowe as she was walking around the counter to straighten up the glove display. He motioned for her to come toward him and leaned down to her ear.

"Mr. Cromwell hasn't been paying on his account. If he wants to buy anything today, it will have to be cash or card only. We can't finance anything more until he's current."

Marlowe nodded. That was the least favorite part of her job. Normally, she didn't work the counter at all. She was usually in the back invoicing and doing paperwork; however, Shanna, the normal clerk, was off today.

Mrs. Cromwell came back in with Mr. Cromwell's wallet, pushing the door with her hip and holding it with her foot for her little one to walk through.

If that wasn't the way it always was, Marlowe might not be so upset about it, but Mr. Cromwell almost acted like he didn't have children.

He never seemed to notice that they were around, and Mrs. Cromwell was always the one carrying them and taking care of them.

It was enough to make any woman cautious. Better to not be married at all than to be married to a miserable jerk who put zero effort into being a good husband and father.

Mrs. Cromwell smiled at her as she walked by, and Marlowe said hi. Then she went back to straightening the gloves.

It was barely five minutes later when the Cromwell family came to the counter to check out, and Marlowe went back behind the counter.

"Did you find everything okay?" she asked Mr. Cromwell pleasantly.

"Where's your free stuff? I didn't find that display."

"That's probably because there isn't one, Mr. Cromwell." Marlowe grabbed the hand scanner and came around the counter to scan the dog food.

"I'll have to file a complaint about that. Get the checkbook out, Inez."

Marlowe's chest eased. She wasn't going to have to confront him about his delinquent account if they were paying for their order with a check.

She came back around and told him the total. "I can print the check from the register if you want me to."

"Oh, that would be great." Mrs. Cromwell looked up and started to hand the check over.

"No. Write it out yourself," Mr. Cromwell commanded.

Marlowe gritted her teeth while trying hard not to look like she was gritting her teeth. The ignorance of the man was so frustrating. He wasn't even trying to be nice.

She supposed there were lots of people in the world like that, but it was hard for her to swallow. Didn't he ever think that he might be a miserable jerk to live with? Did it occur to him that maybe he could try to be nice to his family? Or at least appreciate the fact that he had a pretty amazing wife who was raising fantastic kids and who put up with his selfish jerkishness?

She doubted it. Sometimes, the world just wasn't fair.

The bell tinkled. Marlowe looked up as Mrs. Cromwell finished writing out the check. Her face broke into a grin as Huck held the door and Kylie walked in followed by Clark. Marlowe smiled even bigger as Kylie said very primly, "Thank you, Huck."

She loved that Clark was teaching Huck to hold the door, and she loved that Kylie remembered to say "thank you" without her being there to prompt her. Clark's eyes met hers across the storeroom, and they grinned together. She didn't think about how she knew, but she was sure he was thinking the same thing as she was about the children and their manners.

The kids had been in the store often enough that they knew not to run to her while she was waiting on a customer, and they stayed back with Clark.

The Cromwells left shortly after, with Marlowe making sure to give Mrs. Cromwell an extra smile. She tried to keep the pity off her face while she did so. Everybody had different trials to work through, and dealing with that man on a daily basis with the patience that she showed would form Mrs. Cromwell into a really amazing person. But it still grated on Marlowe's nerves the way that man treated her.

"Jill's not here yet?" Clark asked when they left.

"Nope."

"I figured she would be, since I'm a little late. We had a shoe we couldn't find at home. It was Kylie's, so I wasn't sure whether it was actually in my house or in your house."

Marlowe laughed. "That would be a problem, wouldn't it?"

"It was under my bed," Kylie said with downturned lips, like she was frustrated with herself for losing her shoe.

"It's good you found it. Losing things will happen throughout your life. Might as well accept it and move on." Marlowe wasn't sure that was exactly the right thing to say to her daughter, but some of the tightened lines of Kylie's face eased, so it must have helped a little.

The bell rang again, and Jill walked in.

Jill was as sweet as Dana wasn't, and Marlowe loved her. She wouldn't mind her mother-in-law being just as wonderful. If she ever had a mother-in-law.

The kids ran to her, throwing their arms around her and both of them talking at once about all the things they wanted to do.

Jill came over and chatted for just a bit, but it was a long ride home, and they had a big afternoon planned, so she didn't stay. Kylie hugged Marlowe, and they were soon gone.

"It never gets easier, does it?" Clark said as the door shut behind them, the bell ringing in the silence of the store.

"I think it gets harder," Marlowe said with a sigh. The gloom that almost always settled over her when Kylie walked out weighed heavy on her chest.

"Are you off at three today?"

"Two-thirty, actually."

"I have a couple of errands I need to run—I need to go to the post office and the hardware store—how about I grab some subs and some snack-y things. That'll make it a little easier when we have to face the empty house. Actually, we can go eat them somewhere and put the empty house off even longer."

Marlowe nodded, appreciating his consideration. Of course, it was partly for him too. She knew it was as hard for him to see Huck leave as it was for her to see Kylie go, but still, facing the empty, quiet house was always tough.

"That sounds fantastic." She put her hand on Clark's arm. It wasn't something she normally thought about, but as soon as she did, she was aware of his skin and his heat and his scent in ways that she never had been before.

She tried to push all that aside and to just be sincere with what she wanted to say. "I know you have brothers and friends that you could spend an evening with, and I appreciate you thinking of me and realizing that this is just as hard for me as it is for you. I'm saying it badly... Just... Thank you so much for being so considerate. I appreciate it."

Maybe it was seeing how awful Mr. Cromwell was to his family, and realizing that Clark was his opposite in every way, or maybe it was just the recent storm and the brush with disaster.

"Would you stop being so sappy. You're gonna make me cry." His dimple flashed, and she knew he was joking, mostly.

"There's nothing wrong with men who cry."

"In Missouri, there is."

"Oh, stop it. You can admit that you miss him, and that you're sad that he's gone, and you can also say 'you're welcome' whenever I say thank you for something. There's nothing wrong with admitting that you're doing something nice and accepting my appreciation. Stop being such a man."

"What? You want me to be a woman?" he asked in mock horror. "I'm not one of those people who think that can be changed."

"You would be a really ugly woman. Just saying."

"That does not hurt my feelings. Just so you know it, Low Beam."

"I wasn't trying to hurt your tender feelings, Gable. I was just stating a fact."

"Well, for the record, let me state the fact that I agree with you that I would make a really ugly woman." He wiggled his brows at her. "I also have to say that you would make a really cute guy."

Marlowe's mouth opened and closed. She didn't even know what to say to that. "You are the weirdest person I have ever met. Who says that to people?"

"Would you two stop? You guys hang out in here bickering like children. I mean it's nonstop. There's no rest for the weary." Mr. Long came over to the counter and stood at the end between Marlowe and Clark.

"She started it."

"I did not. You're the one who said I would make a cute guy."

Mr. Long put his hand up. "Marlowe, you are a great employee, until Clark shows up. When he comes in, it's like you become a whole different person, and the responsible, professional adult that works in this store all of a sudden becomes a teenaged girl again."

Marlowe tilted her head and lifted a shoulder. "I'm down for being a teenager again. Maybe nineteen. I like the sound of that age."

"Marlowe, you're completely missing his point. He called you immature." Clark straightened, like making himself taller somehow made him more mature, too. "Grow up."

Mr. Long put both hands on the counter. "It's not just her. You are a responsible man who's in charge of hundreds of acres of agricultural ground and does an amazing job with it every single year, but you act like a simpleton around Marlowe. It ought to be illegal for you two to be around each other."

Mr. Long shook his head, a little smile on his face. Marlowe knew he was just messing with them. Pretty much anyway. The man had been the manager of the store since Clark and she had been toddlers. Every once in a while, he threatened to retire, but she didn't think Clark's family could run the feed store without him.

"Marlowe, you only have fifteen more minutes. Go ahead and go. You were in early a couple of days this week anyway."

Marlowe knew her face brightened. She loved her job, truly, but it was Friday and she'd already watched Huck and Kylie walk away. Now she didn't have to watch Clark go, too. "That's great. Thanks."

"I'll wait in the pickup for you, since you and I shouldn't be seen together. Apparently, there are too many brain cells in the air when you and I get together. Or something like that," Clark said as he winked at Mr. Long and sauntered to the door.

"I don't know whose brain cells they would be, because mine stay in my head, and you don't have any," Marlowe called as she ducked into the office to hang up her vest and gather her things.

Chapter 12

"Whose idea was this?" Marlowe huffed from behind Clark as they climbed the small hill to the remote water tower outside of town.

"Yours," Clark said easily without turning his head to look around at her. After all, he didn't want her to see the smile on his lips. "If it's a bad idea. Mine, if it's a good one."

"Gable. I'm warning you."

"Low Beam, I'm ignoring you."

"Oh my goodness. Would you slow down? I must be really out of shape."

She was kinda huffing. And he was walking faster than he needed to. He was huffing too; he just didn't want her to know it and so had been trying to do it quietly.

He paused for a second, long enough for her to catch up and for him to grab her hand.

That wasn't part of their usual friend routine. He wasn't really sure why he did it. He'd been doing a lot of strange things lately though, and that's what he'd have to blame it on.

Whatever it was, both of them stopped breathing. For what felt like hours but was really only a second or two.

Marlowe swallowed, loud in the outside stillness as her widened eyes looked at the linked hands between them, almost like they weren't theirs. Like those clasped hands were some kind of space rock floating in the air between them.

Clark's eyes dropped, and he looked at their hands, too. He hadn't meant to grab hers, or hadn't thought about grabbing it, but he didn't regret it. He'd spent a lot of time castigating himself for the thoughts he'd been starting to think about Marlowe and worrying about the impact on their friendship.

But today, just before he got into the feed store, as he had Kylie and Huck in his pickup, he'd wondered, maybe he was approaching it from a position of fear.

Maybe he shouldn't live his life from that position.

He never had before.

Being with Marlowe felt right. Not that he thought he should live according to his feelings either. But the Lord had given him a good best friend. Everything he'd ever heard about marriage indicated that the best ones were ones in which the couple were also best friends.

He supposed most people started out with passion and progressed to the friendship and best friend stage.

Maybe he and Marlowe would do it backward.

He kind of wanted to talk to her about it tonight. He supposed holding her hand was maybe a precursor to the conversation he wanted to have. He wasn't sure, based on her current expression, how receptive she was going to be to the idea. But he didn't feel like he could just not do anything. He had to try. Or at least test the waters.

Maybe he'd chicken out. The thought didn't sit well.

He turned, breaking the spell, and tugged on her hand. "Come on. Slowpoke."

"I'm coming, Gable. You're the dingbat that stopped in the middle of the trail."

"I stopped because you asked me to, Slowpoke. Because you couldn't keep up. Apparently, I now not only have to get myself up the trail, but I have to pull you up as well."

"Cool beans. You're pulling me? I'll let you."

He laughed as the tension between their hands increased. "Stop acting like a two-year-old and pull your own weight."

"But you just offered to pull for me."

Clark was so relieved that him grabbing a hold of her hand had not destroyed the comradery between them that he could barely form a coherent thought. He wanted to say something to her about it. Wanted to say "thank you for not making this awkward." But he didn't want to bring any more attention to it than what he had to.

Baby steps.

The trail wound around the hill and a couple big rocks before the water tower came into sight.

"There it is. Not much longer, Low Beam."

"It's a good thing because you're starting to slow down. I thought I was going to have to start pushing you up the hill. Hardly fair since you're bigger."

"Life is not fair, Low Beam. You shoulda figured that out by now."

"Well, it's not fair for the rest of the world, but between you and me, things can be fair."

"That's pie-in-the-sky thinking, Sweetie. Things are never fair. Never meaning never, not never meaning except for between us. It means never."

"Wow. Someone's really pessimistic today."

"Am I wrong?"

"Well, yeah. Of course, you're wrong. Because if you're wrong, that means I'm right."

"That's interesting." He held up the bag he was carrying. "Then why am I carrying this, and you're carrying nothing? That's not fair."

"Yes, it is. You have more muscles than I do. So it's perfectly fair that you carry more weight."

"Do you have to argue with everything I say?"

"I do argue a lot, don't I?" Her voice was a little more subdued, and he should've known better than to say something about it. He knew that was one of her sore spots. One that she was trying to work on.

"I'm sorry. I shouldn't have said that. You don't argue too much. You and I were just messing around."

"I know you didn't mean it. I just know it's something I need to work on."

Her voice still wasn't back to the perky way it had been before he'd stupidly hit her where it hurt, and they didn't say anything more until they reached the water tower.

It wasn't the safest thing they'd ever done, but there was a ladder that went up to a platform where they could sit with their legs hanging down and look across the valley. The sunsets were spectacular up there, and it was quiet and peaceful.

They'd spent plenty of time up there over the years. It was the perfect place for him to talk to her.

"You first," he said as he stood beside the ladder and tugged her toward it.

She glanced at his eyes and put one hand on the ladder. He didn't want to make it awkward, but he did hold on to her hand a second or two longer than maybe he should have.

Something flashed in her eyes. He wasn't sure what it was. He was hopeful that it was not irritation, but more of a maybe-I'm-interested-in-my-best-friend-as-more-than-a-best-friend.

What would he know about it though? He'd been kinda dumb when it came to girls. He'd definitely been dumb when it came to choosing a wife.

He pulled his hand back, and she looked to the ladder, putting her hand on and climbing up. He climbed up after her, careful to keep the bag from bouncing around too much. He didn't want their subs to be smashed.

It didn't take long to get settled on the platform and get their food out. They munched in silence for a while. Companionable silence. He couldn't think of too many times where they'd had an awkward silence.

"Did the insurance adjuster come back with a quote for you?"

The adjuster had been there earlier in the week, but the man had said he needed to go back to the office and run some figures before he'd know for sure.

"No. But I told him that my case didn't need to be a rush thing. That all the people who were living in shelters could be ahead of me. I know we talked about it. I hope that was still okay?"

"Yeah." He wanted to say something about living with her being better than he thought it would be or being everything he thought it would be... He didn't know. Something. To let her know that he enjoyed sharing a house, a home, with her.

That would lead nicely into the conversation that he wanted to have about them being more than friends, but he couldn't think of any way to start it off. So he kept his mouth shut.

There weren't too many times in his life where he'd been nervous to the point of losing his appetite, but he only ate half of the sub before he wrapped it up and put it away.

"Are you sick?" Marlowe asked.

He should've known she'd notice. Of course she knew how much he usually ate.

"Did you eat before?"

"No." His stomach cramped. Again, here was an opportunity to start the conversation he wanted to have, but how?

He should just come out and say it. What to say? Or maybe the question wasn't what to say, maybe the question was more how did he get over his fear.

"Then why aren't you eating?" Now there was concern in her voice, and she turned her head to look at him.

There was a bag of potato chips between them, and he was tempted to pick them up and move them out of the way. Because he wanted to be closer.

That was probably premature.

He swallowed, supposing this was the best opening he was going to get.

"Last weekend, I guess maybe it started with the tornado, but when Dana came, she started talking about custody and how she was married..."

His voice trailed off, and he tried to figure out how he wanted to say the next part.

But Marlowe wasn't stupid; she was pretty astute actually. And she spoke, softly and a little hesitantly. "Are you talking about what we didn't talk about?"

Maybe with somebody else, he would've tilted his head and wondered what in the world they were saying, but Marlowe hit it exactly right. Although he supposed he should say the words out loud.

"Yeah. When we looked at each other, I think both of us were thinking the same thing."

"Yeah. I think we were." She bit her lip. Her brows were drawn down a little, and he knew she was worried about the same thing that made his stomach twist and burn.

He could quit this conversation right now, and maybe everything would go back to the way it was.

But he'd realized he wasn't happy with the way things were. He wanted more. He could only hope that if Marlowe didn't want more now, she would think about it and realize that maybe eventually she would.

"I thought... I was thinking, that we could... That if we... That we might solve the problem, if we..."

Why was the M-word so hard to say?

"Married. We were both thinking that we could get married and solve the Dana problem, and some other problems while we're at it. Like the fact that Huck doesn't have a mother, at his house anyway, and that Kylie doesn't have a father at all. And that you fill that role perfectly for her."

"Yeah. That's exactly what I was thinking. We could get married."

She sighed and looked off into the distance. The sun was going down, and long shadows draped across the hill from the few trees. Brown fields already planted and holding the seed full of ripened grain come September stretched out into the distance. Dark brown, deep and rich. Good soil, and some of it was his.

He wasn't rich though. He couldn't flaunt that in front of her or use that to try to convince her. Not that Marlowe would be swayed by such a thing. He knew her well enough to know that.

What he owned didn't matter to her, although he supposed what he did *would* matter. If he worked hard and was poor, he was pretty sure she'd be okay with it. She knew agriculture was not a guarantee and often volatile.

"You said that's where it started? Where what started?" She didn't look at him as she spoke, her gaze scanning the horizon and her half-eaten sub sitting in her lap with her fingernail picking at a piece of the crust.

He took a deep breath. He needed to be brave. "I'm gonna say something, something I considered not saying, because I don't want to ruin anything."

She held a hand up. "Could you wait? I have something I need to say first."

That wasn't what he was expecting. "Um, yeah. I guess."

"I don't know what you're going to say, but I've been thinking about something this week...something that happened a long time ago, and I know I never told you about it, and I feel like I need to confess it."

Chapter 13

Clark held his hand up. "On second thought, let me go first, please."

Marlowe bit her tongue. She thought it would be easier for her to make sure she got out what she wanted to say first. Or maybe not easier, but better, although she truly had no idea what Clark was going to say.

She was worried he was going to say they needed to put distance between them, or he'd found someone to date, or since he had thought of marriage with her, he figured out someone else he wanted to be married to and was going to start seeing her. Although Marlowe would have no idea who that was. There were several eligible ladies in town, and any one of them might be interested in Clark.

All of them knew what a great dad he was, and he was good-looking and funny too.

She pushed back her nerves and tried for humor. "Sure, Gable. Ladies first off the *Titanic*, men first the rest of the time."

"Very funny, Low Beam. If you want to go first, go ahead."

"No, really. I insist. You." She wrapped up her sandwich and crossed her arms over her chest.

"You."

"No, you."

"Rock, paper, scissors?" he asked with more than a little humor in his tone.

"Okay. It's the only fair way."

"There are no fair ways," he said as he held his fist up with hers.

They said it together, "rock, paper, scissors, shoot!" They yelled the "shoot" together as their fists bumped down.

He did rock, but she did paper, because she knew he always did rock first.

"Best two out of three?" he asked with a look that said he knew he'd lost.

She rolled her eyes. "Don't be ridiculous. I won. So you go first."

"I thought you won, so you go first."

"Just talk, Gable. I know you're a man, so this is kinda complicated, but it's where you open your mouth and words come out."

"Could you explain that again, only this time number the steps and say it slower, please?"

She laughed and shook her head. The sun had started to touch the horizon, and pink and light blue were stretched out across the sky. Pretty.

"Sure," she said. "Start talking, or I'll push you off the water tower. How's that?"

"Whoa." He looked over between his knees at the ground. "That's a long way down. Would you really push me off?"

"Or you could start talking so we don't have to find out how mean I really am."

"Oh, I already know how mean you really are."

She crossed her arms over her chest. "What's that supposed to mean?" Then she dropped her arms and held her hand up. "Never mind. Ignore that. Just speak. What were you going to say that was so hard for you to say that you were mumbling and stumbling around?"

"Wow, that bad?"

She nodded.

"Okay." He rubbed his hands together and swung his feet so they kicked back and forth below the platform. Normally, Clark didn't have a hard time sitting still, so she knew he was pretty worked up about this. Probably, if she had to guess, because he was afraid of her reaction.

She just hoped he didn't say he thought she needed to move out. And she really hoped he didn't say he wanted to date someone else. Which was weird, because that had never bothered her before.

"I want us to be more than friends."

Her mouth dropped. It didn't hit the ground, but it felt close.

She had not been expecting that. Not really. Actually, not at all. And maybe her stunned silence said that. She tried to process it, but the words just weren't computing in her brain.

Maybe she was quiet too long, because he spoke again. "I mean, I'd like to try it. You know, like maybe we can date or something..." His voice trailed off.

He slapped his hands down on the platform, and she almost thought he was going to get up. But he didn't.

"Never mind. That was stupid. I don't know why I'm even thinking that way. I don't want to ruin the great friendship that we have."

"So... What made you think of this?" She drew the words out, because what she really wanted to know was whether he wanted to be more than friends because he liked her, or because they both thought that it would be a good thing and solve a lot of problems for them to get married.

"I don't know." He brushed his hands down his legs.

She couldn't expect him to talk if she couldn't get the words out. "Is this just because you think it's a good idea for us to get married?"

Wow, that was a hard sentence to say. Her chest felt heavy and twisted as she waited on his answer.

"No." The word was soft, and his eyes followed the sunset, which spread across the sky in brilliant orange, pink, and flaming red. "It's because... Listen, if I'm being an idiot, you can just tell me. But since we were in the basement together during the storm, I've had a hard time making my eyes do anything but sit on you when you're around. I found myself wanting to touch you, and that's not something I've ever had any thoughts about before. I keep waiting for the adrenaline to wear off, but I'm pretty sure it's not adrenaline." His Adam's apple bobbed, and he looked down at his hands. "I'm sorry if this makes you uncomfortable."

He drew in and blew out a shaky breath, and she wasn't sure she'd ever seen him more nervous. Well, maybe one time, when he was competing in the state youth tractor driving championship.

She wanted to ease his misery. Maybe she could, just by being honest.

She clasped her hands tightly together and put her words out into the evening air. "I've been having the same problem. It started the same time. Although, what I thought I should confess to you goes along with that."

"Well, I've got mine out, and you haven't pushed me off the platform, so I think I'm doing good. Go ahead and hit me with yours."

She didn't move, suddenly finding her hands very interesting. "Back in high school, the group of girls that I ran with, there were like five of us. We had a slumber party one night, and we voted you the boy in high school with the most kissable lips. Ever since then, I've wondered what it would be like to kiss my best friend."

The last words came out fast, and she had her head down, because she wanted to squirm, like there were worms or snakes in her stomach. That was about the stupidest thing she'd ever said in her life before.

No, not about, it *was* the stupidest thing she'd ever said. As soon as the words hit the evening air and hung there, she wished she could take them back. There was no need for her to say it.

"Funny you should admit that now. That was years ago."

"This week, the memory has been stronger. I've been thinking about it a lot."

She just kept getting dumber and dumber.

He laughed a little. "So let me get this straight, you and your friends voted me the guy with the most kissable lips in school?"

She nodded without looking at him. Miserable.

"I didn't even know there was such a thing." His voice faded before he spoke again. "That happened how many years ago? And you never told me?" He leaned forward and over a little, tilting his head and trying to meet her eyes. "Low Beam. Hello? You gonna look at me, or you gonna sit there and stare at your hands all night?"

"Stop it. I didn't make fun of you."

"I didn't say anything that shocking." He poked her leg with his finger. "And I've only been keeping my secret for a week. You're going on what? Like a decade and half?"

"A lot of things have happened in those almost-fifteen years. It wasn't like I thought about it every day or anything." Finally, she looked up, irritated. "I don't know why you're giving me such a hard time. You said you want to be more than friends. You do know that includes kissing?"

"No? Really?"

She could definitely hear the humor in his voice.

His dimple flashed. "I mean, I thought we would start kind of slow. Like maybe we'd hold hands tonight or something. I wasn't thinking of a big make-out session on top of the water tower like right now." He huffed a little and maybe snorted. "But I guess I do have kissable lips, so if you can't control yourself, have at 'em."

She laughed in spite of herself. "I've managed to control myself for the last decade and a half or so, pretty sure I can do so again tonight. I just always kind of wondered."

"Well, Low Beam, don't wander too far, you might get lost."

"That's what I brought you along for. I don't have to worry about where we're going, as long as you're around. You'll get us home."

"That must be nice. Freeloading on my brainpower. You ought to have a job of your own or something."

"I've cooked for you all week. Surely that counts for something. I cook; when we go out, you make sure we get back. That seems like a fair trade."

"Hmmm. I'll have to think on that. Maybe I owe you. You cook every day, I only use my homing instincts once in a while, so it doesn't really seem fair."

"Life isn't fair. The Great Gable says that all the time. Or maybe it's Gable the Great."

"I've had that nickname for twenty-five years; you can't change it now. It's Gable, and that's it."

"Twenty-five years? Aren't we exaggerating just a little? I'm pretty sure I didn't watch *Gone with the Wind* when I was three years old."

"Really? We're gonna quibble over details?"

"Yeah, I'll quibble over anything right now just to change the subject." She put her hands on her cheeks. They were still hot. "It's going to be a long time before I'm not embarrassed about this anymore."

"About what? Voting me the most kissable lips?" He bumped her shoulder with his. "Hey, was that vote unanimous?"

"Would you believe me if I said I cast the one dissenting vote?" She bit her lip and looked at him. Maybe she could get out of this after all.

"Nope. I bet you were the one that nominated me."

"No. Now that I did not do."

"Then who did you nominate?"

She pushed her hair over her shoulder, figuring she could give him a few seconds to squirm or at least wait. Then she admitted, "No one. When Janice suggested you, I certainly couldn't argue with her."

There. She admitted it. All of it. But she couldn't even think of another guy. Clark might be her best friend, but he was still perfect—right up to his lips.

He leaned back, putting his hands on the boards behind him and looking at the sky as the color slowly faded into a deep pink and orange just along the far horizon.

"So, how curious are you?"

"About what?" She imitated him, leaning back on her hands too. There was a chip bag between their legs, but their pinky fingers touched.

"Kissing me."

"Are you speaking in the present tense?"

"Yeah."

"Can't we talk about you for a little bit?" She didn't give him time to answer. "So, what exactly were you thinking this week?" That was a really awkward subject change, but at least it got the pressure off her—as long as he went with it.

"I was thinking that I was stupid when I married Dana, and that you would make some guy a perfect wife, and I kind of wanted that guy to be me."

His words took her breath away, and it took her a minute to suck air back into her lungs. Another minute passed before she felt she could speak in a calm tone. "And kissing never entered your thoughts?"

"I can't say that."

"Then what can you say?"

His pinky finger rubbed against hers, and she felt that touch the whole way up her arm. It shot through her chest and ran down both legs. Inside her shoes, her toes curled.

"Every time I saw you, I wanted to touch you. You have that dip in your waist, and I kept thinking I'd like to rest my hand right there. No, my hands. One on each side. Then I could pull you closer."

He stopped talking, so she said, "Is this where we get to the kissing part?"

"Holy smokes, you're impatient. No way. I'm not ready to kiss yet. I just barely touched your waist. There's a lot of other places I want to touch before I kiss you."

"Really?"

"Sure. I've never touched your hair. Well, I've probably touched it, but I think I'd like to run my hands through it." He raised a brow at her. "I got the plural first time that time."

"I noticed. You're improving. Go on."

"Go on? Like, keep talking?"

"Yeah. What else? I want to get to the kissing part."

"I haven't watched that many romance movies. Only the ones you forced me into. I want action. There isn't going to be a kissing part."

"No kissing?" She put her lip out in a pout. "I thought you said there was kissing?"

"No, that was you. You're all about the kissing."

"I'm pretty sure you said something about kissing."

"Maybe I changed my mind. Or maybe you misheard me."

"No. I didn't mishear you. You said kissing. I definitely heard it."

"I'm pretty sure you said kissing too. Maybe I want to hear about your kissing."

"No way. You've left us standing face-to-face with your hands in my hair. I want to hear the rest."

Most of the light had faded from the sky, and there was just a dim glow, but she could see his features easily when he turned his face toward hers.

"I don't think I want to talk about it."

She knew he didn't mean to hurt her, but it did. It was like he was shutting her out.

"I think I'd rather show you."

Oh.

Well.

"Okay."

His grin was slow and easy, and if she felt his touch clear to her toes, that grin went straight to her heart, burning the whole way.

"I think I have to stand up for this."

She looked over the edge of the water tank, wondering.

Then she looked behind them. If she stretched her head as far as she could, she could touch the water tank, just brushing it. There wasn't much room on the platform.

"Do you think it's dangerous?"

"Us kissing? What dangerous thing do you think is going to happen?"

"Well, I don't know what kind of kisser you are. We might fall off the platform. That would be kind of an inauspicious beginning."

"All right, you talked me into it. We'll do this sitting down."

That wasn't exactly what she'd meant. "Maybe we should get off the water tower. And do it on the ground."

"You stalling?"

"I'm just trying to be safe."

"If we were being safe, we wouldn't have had this discussion to begin with. We definitely wouldn't be thinking about kissing each other."

"Good point. I was talking about physical safety."

"Oh, boy." He sounded truly distressed. "That means you probably had a bigger influence on me than I like to admit, if I'm concerned about our emotions." He huffed out a breath. "That's scary."

"That *is* scary. I might have to rethink this. I'm not sure I want a man who is that in touch with his feminine side."

"I'm not sure I want a woman who's not sure she wants me."

"Seriously? You left us standing there with your hands in my hair facing each other, and now you're not even sure whether you want me or not? I never got to the kissing part. You can't dump me without kissing me first."

"You're not making any sense." His hand reached up and cupped her cheek, sliding along it, and she pressed her head into his palm. "It's a new side of you. I think I kinda like it."

"I just hope it doesn't last. I need my brain. It feels like mush right now." Her words were whispered and soft, and they faded off completely as he moved his hand around her head.

Chapter 14

Clark leaned on his elbow, running his other hand through Marlowe's hair. "I can't believe how perfect this feels."

"My hair?" Marlowe asked with one of her little grins. The kind that said she knew that wasn't what he was talking about but she was being goofy. He definitely liked goofy Marlowe.

"Well, your hair does seem perfect. But what I really meant was being here with you. I can't believe I didn't see this before."

She wiggled just a little closer and rolled to her side too. "This feels like more stalling on your part. I'm starting to really be afraid that I'm not going to get kissed tonight."

"It's our first kiss. Don't rush it."

"Gable. It is not our first kiss."

He laughed. "Seriously? What were we? Four? Six? You can't count that atrocity of a kiss as our first kiss? Please don't. That's not a good memory."

"It was a little offensive at the time, because I'm pretty sure you threw up on me. But it's kind of funny now."

"If you say so."

"I do. So that takes all the pressure of the first kiss off." She paused before adding, a little breathlessly, he thought, "We can rush."

"Maybe I don't want to."

She put a hand on his waist and wiggled just a little closer. Close enough that their breath mingled and he could feel the heat from her body. It wasn't quite close enough, because they weren't touching.

She lifted her brows at him and said softly, "Then maybe I ought to take charge of the situation. You've had plenty of time, and you're wasting it."

He slid his hand down, and she felt soft and warm. He slid it around her back and pulled her closer, enough to erase the distance between them. "Can't you let a man enjoy this?"

"I hope."

Her words were a little flippant, but there was a note of insecurity there, and he lowered his head. He didn't want her to be insecure about how he felt, even if he probably wasn't going to be the best at saying the words. He figured he could show her, and that might help negate his inability to articulate his feelings with any degree of depth.

"Oh, I guarantee it." He couldn't keep from smiling, which might not have been the most romantic thing in the world to do, but she smiled as well, and it felt right again. They were friends first. Best friends. Part of their friendship had always been being able to laugh with each other. Although, he did want her to understand that he was serious, not just about this, but about her.

"Are you going to stop moving those things long enough for me to kiss them?"

After raising her brows, she puckered her lips and closed her eyes.

He wanted to be serious, but he couldn't help but laugh. "That wasn't the kind of kiss I was thinking about, but it'll do for a start."

He bent down and touched her lips with his, softly, just a light touch. Another little brush and again, and by the third time, he pulled her closer and pressed harder, and her lips had softened under his, and he was finally kissing her the way he wanted.

It caught him off guard when she pressed against him, pushing him down on his back, without breaking contact, and she had both his cheeks in her hands, and her hair was a veil around them, and her scent was filling his senses and closing out the rest of the world, and all he could feel was her body warm and hard and right on his, and all he wanted was to be closer and to stay like that forever, with the soft night air and the spinning in space and the pounding of his blood and Marlowe the only solid anchor.

It was a long time later when she finally lifted her head and pressed her cheek against his, her hand in his hair and her breath in his ear.

She'd changed his world. It was completely different. Better. In every way better.

There was too much going through his head and his body for him to be able to say the romantic words she probably deserved.

But he could think of something, and maybe he shouldn't have said it, but he whispered in her ear, "That was a heck of a lot better than last time."

Her laugh puffed in his ear, and she lifted her head enough for their noses to touch. "You've gotten a little better yourself there, Gable."

His breath felt shaky, and he didn't want to use her nickname. It just didn't seem as serious as he wanted to be. "Marlowe, I... I..." He was on the verge of saying he thought he was falling in love with her. He thought she'd be okay with it. But it felt a little soon. And so he said the only other thing he could think of. "I'd like to do that again."

Maybe "I love you" would've been better, but what came out made her smile and lower her head, so he figured it wasn't too bad.

~~~

Monday evening, Marlowe stood in the kitchen chopping chicken for the casserole she was making for supper.

All day, she'd had so much trouble getting the silly grin off her face. But now, she was having trouble keeping her foot still and her stomach from twisting like a crushed soda can.

Saturday night had been a bit magical. Sunday morning, they'd gone to church and sat together, which definitely raised a few eyebrows. Usually, Marlowe and Kylie sat in the seat in front of Clark and Huck. Sitting together in church was almost like announcing to the town that they were engaged.

Except, they weren't.

Marlowe wasn't sure exactly what they were. They hadn't really talked about it other than being "more" than friends. How much more? What was that called?

The kids had come home Sunday evening, and things had been crazy, trying to get clothes washed and unpacked and things ready for school in the morning, with Clark having to start work before daylight on Monday morning so she'd taken the kids to school.

He'd texted her that he'd be home in time for supper though, and she wasn't sure how they were going to play this in front of the children. She wasn't sure exactly what "this" was.

Were they telling the children? If they were, what, exactly, were they telling the children? She chewed on her lip and tried to concentrate on the chicken so she didn't end up getting a piece of her finger in it, too.

She supposed it would just play out, and she really didn't need to worry.

Even as she thought that, she set the knife down and rinsed her hands off, drying them on the towel before picking up her phone.

What are we doing about the children?

There. Just asking him made her feel better.

What happened with the kids?

Okay. She thought he'd know exactly what she meant, but apparently not.

Nothing. I meant about us. What are we doing about us with the kids?

This time, his reply took a little longer.

Um, I'm not sure what exactly you're asking?

She looked at her phone in frustration. How could she say that any more clearly?

Before she thought of anything, her phone buzzed again.

I'm here. Can I come in, and we'll talk about it?

Now he was asking permission to come into his own house. She had to laugh. She knew he wasn't afraid of her, so she wasn't sure what brought that on.

Yes.

Maybe he was as uncertain as she was. Or maybe he seriously didn't know what she was talking about.

She hadn't wanted to let the chicken just sit on the counter. By the time she got it scraped off the cutting board and her hands rinsed off again, he was already at the door.

She held the towel that she'd been drying her hands off with and stood in front of him, three feet away, as he walked in.

Their eyes met. Hers were happy, she was sure, but also uncertain. Kylie didn't have a dad, and she absolutely adored Clark, so Marlowe wasn't worried about her reaction to finding out about any kind of relationship Clark and she might have.

And what was their relationship, exactly?

But Huck might be a different story. He had a mom. Although he probably didn't remember his mom and dad ever living together, she figured, like most kids, he probably hoped they would. Or at least he wished for it.

Clark might not want to spring things on them too fast.

She'd try not to push and just let Clark lead. It was his child that had the most at stake.

She stopped thinking when he spoke. "Is it sappy for me to say I missed you today?"

"It probably is. But I like hearing it." She couldn't keep her lips from curving up.

He took a step toward her. "I missed you today."

"I think you just said that."

"No, I asked if it was okay for me to say it. I didn't actually say it. Until just now."

She shook her head; in his crazy way, he could always make her laugh. She was really glad to know that their kiss hadn't changed that.

"I thought about kissing you a lot too."

"That's what I was asking. Are you okay with the kids seeing us?"

"I can't imagine they'd be anything but happy. We've kinda been mom and dad to them just living in separate houses for years now."

She couldn't keep from biting her lip. "But...what are we, exactly? I mean, I don't want to push you into anything, and I guess I'm not sure myself..." Had their relationship shifted? She thought it had, but she needed to know what he was thinking about it.

He blinked a little, like it hadn't occurred to him that they needed to define anything. His hand came up and cupped her cheek. "What do you want?"

"I want to know what you're thinking."

"Do I have to think?" he asked, and immediately looked like he wished he could take it back. "I'm sorry. You need me to be serious, and here I am joking and goofing off."

"Yes." She didn't even smile. "I need you to be serious."

"I think you know I like kissing you, and I think you like it too. So...that's more than friends...are we a couple? I'm okay with that."

She nodded. Relief making her chest feel light. That's what she'd thought, too.

"Maybe we'll just go slow for a little bit and see...I think I know exactly what I want, but I want you to be sure. We don't want to screw things up for the kids."

"That's what I was asking. What are we doing in front of the kids?"

She didn't get to say anything more about it, because Huck came running out to the kitchen yelling for his dad, and Kylie trailed behind, until Clark had a kid on each side with their arms wrapped around his waist.

It was a sight that made Marlowe's heart swell. She started to turn back toward the cutting board where she'd left off from supper.

"Hey. Hold off there a minute." He stepped forward as the kids' arms dropped from him, until he was in front of her, and one of his hands came and slipped around her neck. "Are you okay with it?"

She nodded.

His lips split into another grin. "Good." He didn't say anything else, but his head leaned down, and he kissed her, right there in the kitchen. It might not have been a kiss quite as heart-stopping as the one they shared on top of the water tower, but it was enough to make Marlowe feel like she needed to grab for the counter to steady herself when he pulled back.

"Eww. You guys are kissing. That's gross." Huck's cute little voice cut through the fog that surrounded Marlowe's brain.

"You know, son, when I was your age, I thought the exact same thing. Since Marlowe's grown up, though, she's gotten a little better at it, and it's not quite so bad."

Huck wrinkled his nose.

Marlowe put her free hand on her hip. "I know for a fact that kissing you was gross when you were that age. And you've gotten a little bit better at it too."

"I'm pretty sure you said I got a lot better."

"Oh really?" She raised her brows. "I can't remember." And with a little sassy swing of her chin, she turned and went back to her supper preparations.

Chapter 15

Friday afternoon, Marlowe was just leaving the feed store when she got a call on her cell phone. She stopped on the sidewalk beside her car and answered. It was a number she didn't recognize.

"Hello?"

"Ms. Glass?" a slightly older male voice said.

"Yes?" She kinda suspected that it might be a call from the insurance adjuster. It had been slightly odd that she hadn't heard anything from him, but she had told him to put her case on last.

"This is Mr. Bill Sanders, your insurance adjuster. I was out there ten or so days ago, to look at your house."

"Yes sir, I remember."

"I didn't say this at the time, but there was significant structural damage, and I was pretty sure that we were going to be tearing it down and building a new one. I had to get the final go-ahead from my boss, but the way your house is built, there's just one crossbeam, and it was cracked significantly. We could have braced it, but I wouldn't trust that."

He paused, so Marlowe said, "Okay?"

He huffed a little. Maybe a laugh. "What that means is I'm going to be giving you a rather large check. Obviously, you can bulldoze the house and rebuild if you want. Or you can relocate. Since you don't have a mortgage, you don't absolutely have to use the money to rebuild the house. It's up to you."

Marlowe couldn't think of what else she would do with it, except…a thought popped into her head. She'd always wanted to go back and finish college, but she'd struggled with being a single mom, worrying about taking care of Kylie and working and studying.

She'd never wanted to be in debt, which was why she'd spent two years working before she started college to begin with.

Maybe this was God opening that door for her. Finally.

What timing. She thought about Clark. They'd never talked any more about the relationship, other than they weren't going to hide it from their children. She supposed both of them were a little wary about having a relationship with each other while they were living in the same house. It was a recipe for disaster. But they hadn't talked about that, either.

She wanted to talk to Clark about it right away, but she knew he was supposed to be late getting home tonight. The corn was mostly planted, and he had been spraying. With the rain that was forecast to move in tomorrow, he wasn't going to want to stop until he absolutely had to. They only had a short window after the corn was planted to get the field sprayed.

"Thank you."

"I'll be emailing you my estimate, you can take a look over it, and if it suits you, you have to sign it and send it back to me. Then we'll cut your check. Over and done. That easy."

"Thanks." She pushed the red button and turned to her car.

Whatever she was getting would almost assuredly be enough for her to pay to finish her degree and get her master's, which would enable her to get a really fantastic job. She'd be able to take care of Kylie easily, maybe even send her to private school.

They'd have to move away for her to go to school, and also for her to get a good-paying job, as there was no such thing around here.

Since the tree had fallen, she'd pretty much come to grips that she'd be losing her house – the place where she'd grown up and her last real connection to her mom and sister. It wasn't as hard as it might have been. After all, she'd spent almost as much time in Clark's home as she had in her own, and Clark had been able to get everything with sentimental value out. That wasn't the problem.

Did she really want to move?

She and Clark could still have a relationship. Of course. But it would be a long-distance one, since there really weren't any colleges around that she could commute to. She would have to move. Of course.

Well, she didn't have to make that decision right now. She wouldn't be seeing Clark tonight anyway. At least not until late, if he did come home.

She drove to the school, picked the kids up, and listened to them chat about their days and to each other on the ride home.

She didn't want to pull into the driveway when she came over the rise and saw Dana's car parked in front of Clark's house.

But being an adult meant that she couldn't play hooky—that's what it would be—from going home. So she pulled in beside Dana's car and helped the children out. They ran into the house with her following along more slowly.

She'd barely gotten in the house, was still closing the door behind her, when Dana confronted her in the kitchen. "I'm taking Huck with me. I'll have him back by bedtime."

Marlowe stopped, still holding onto the doorknob. "Did you talk to Clark about this?"

She knew Clark was busy, but usually he was pretty good at texting her about any plans for the children. She couldn't imagine that he wouldn't have said something about this.

"I'm his mother. I didn't see him last weekend, so obviously, it's perfectly fine for me to see him now. Clark's not even here. If I know him, since it's not raining, he'll be out in the field somewhere puttering around."

Marlowe clamped her teeth together and tried to keep a pleasant expression on her face. Clark was out in the field, working his butt off, putting in long hours, and growing grain on hundreds of acres. It wasn't like he was out playing, the way Dana insinuated. It made her mad that Dana would dismiss what Clark did with such a blasé ignorance.

"I'll text him now and make sure it's okay. I really don't have the authority to give permission for Huck to leave." She pulled her phone out and started typing on it.

"Don't get smart with me. I know what's going on between you two. I think it's pretty sad that you're doing this right under the nose of my son."

Marlowe hit send and blinked at her phone several times, taking several measured breaths. Dana didn't really believe what she was saying; she didn't see anything wrong with what she was insinuating was going on between Clark and Marlowe. But Marlowe supposed she'd lived in a small town long enough to know that that was an area where she could hit Marlowe and possibly score points.

Maybe if she and Clark were actually doing what Dana had insinuated, it would have.

"I just sent a text. Hopefully he'll reply shortly."

She tried to remember if he was working in the one field where they didn't have very good reception. She didn't think so. And sure enough, his text came back right away.

I guess if she has to. I can't really stop her. Did she say where she was taking him?

"He was just wondering where you're going to take Huck?"

"I don't have to tell him."

"No. Of course not. But it's probably a smart idea to at least let him know where you're going to be. That way if anything happens, we know where to start looking for you. Just as a safety precaution." It seemed like common sense to Marlowe, but she also knew so often divorce seemed to eradicate common sense.

"Nothing's going to happen. But if you want to talk to your boyfriend some more, you can tell him that I've spoken with my lawyer, and we will be filing papers for me to get full custody." Her lips smiled, but her eyes were shrewd. "He said since I was married and can provide a much more stable home for my little Huck, that there was every possibility that a judge would grant me the full custody that I deserve." Her nose wrinkled a little before she turned. "Huck, darling? Oh, Hucky. Darling little boy, come to Mommy. We're going for a little ridey."

Marlowe's knuckles were white as she gripped her phone. How was she going to tell this to Clark? Should she say it in such a way that he was alarmed and possibly came immediately? Or should she reassure him and try to make sure her words were not incendiary?

She wished she could keep her bias out of it, but there had to be some kind of bias. She couldn't clinically tell him that she thought his ex-wife was trying to steal his son.

Maybe that was a little too dramatic.

At the very least, if they went to court, Clark would lose the full custody he had with permitted visits.

Finally, she decided to just be as honest as she could.

She won't say where she's going, but she said she should have him back by bedtime.

She hesitated a bit before she hit send. The idea that Dana had gone to a lawyer was definitely something she wanted to tell Clark, but it probably didn't fit into this conversation. She hoped she was making the right decision.

Thanks.

He didn't say more. She set her phone down.

Huck, with Kylie at his side, came walking back through the living room and into the kitchen. He stopped in front of Marlowe. "Is Dad going to be here when I get back?"

It figured this would happen in the busiest time of year. She sighed. "I think so. He's planning on it."

"But you will be, right?"

She nodded. "I'll be here."

The golden bracelets on Dana's wrist clanked together as she put a skinny arm around Huck. "Come on now, sweetie. I have a special surprise for you. And I know you're going to love this. You and Mommy are going to have a really great time together." She opened the door and walked out without a backward glance.

Marlowe closed it behind her. The house seemed unnaturally quiet.

She'd almost forgotten about Kylie until her daughter spoke from behind her. "She is going to bring him back, isn't she?"

Marlowe wanted to say a definite yes. But she also didn't want her daughter to have this memory etched in her head, one of her mother lying, in case Huck didn't come back. So she had to be honest. "I hope so."

She was just about ready to tell Kylie that maybe they could do something special this evening since it was just them home alone, for the first time since the storm, when her phone rang.

"I have some fruit on a tray in the fridge if you want to grab it for a little snack," she said before she answered the call. It was Emma, Clark's mother. "Hello?"

"Marlowe. I hope I've caught you at a good time. I just had a quick question."

"Yeah. I'm not busy."

"Well, I was really calling about Kylie. I know Dana's in town. She was talking at the diner while I was in with Walter, and she said she was taking Huck for the evening. I wasn't really eavesdropping; she was just talking in the booth right behind me. Anyway, I knew Kylie and you would probably be alone this evening. I didn't know if it would be okay if I took Kylie, and she and I could do something? That would give you a little time for yourself."

Marlowe didn't have to think about it. "She would love that. Thank you so much for offering, Mrs. Hudson. I can bring her to meet you if you want me to." Marlowe didn't have to even ask Kylie. She'd spent plenty of time with Mrs. Hudson, who was like a grandmother to her. Marlowe knew she'd be over the moon to spend the evening with her.

"Oh no, honey, you don't have to do that. I was just out delivering supper to the guys that are in the field, and I can swing by and pick her up. I'll have her back by nine or so this evening. I think we'll have a girls' night and give ourselves mannies and peddies and watch a movie."

"Kylie will love it. Thanks."

"Perfect. Will she be ready in ten minutes?"

"Yes. We'll wait on the porch."

They hung up. And as she suspected, Kylie was staring at her, waiting to pounce as soon as her phone hit the counter. "Who was it, Mommy? What's happening? What will I like?"

It was as excited as Kylie got, since she was usually very mature and serious for a five-year-old. It made Marlowe smile to see her animation.

"Grandma Hudson is gonna take you and spend some time with you this evening. I think she said you guys are going to paint your nails and watch a movie. I'm sure there's going to be food involved, too."

"Yay!" Kylie jumped up and down and waved the apple slice in her hand.

True to her word, Mrs. Hudson pulled in nine and a half minutes later.

Kylie hadn't needed that much time to get everything ready to go, and she was waiting at the door. She squealed when Mrs. Hudson pulled in and went running out the door. Marlowe walked out to the porch and stood at the top of the stairs with her hand on the post while Kylie ran to Mrs. Hudson and wrapped her arms around the older lady.

Despite having raised five boys, Mrs. Hudson still looked young and was slender but not skinny. She chatted with Kylie for a couple of minutes, then stepped back, and her little dog, some kind of poodle mix, hopped out of her car. Kylie took off running around the house with it.

Mrs. Hudson closed her door and started toward the steps. "I hope you don't mind, I told Kylie she could run around with Gracie for a little bit. Do you have a minute to chat?"

"I sure do. All of the sudden, I have a completely free evening in front of me. Would you like to come in for a cup of coffee and a snack?"

"Oh no, honey. You don't have to do that. But I told you I was delivering meals to the boys, and I talked to Clark for a little bit." She gave a little smile, and Marlowe figured she knew what was coming. Clark must've told her.

Mrs. Hudson made it to the top of the steps, and Marlowe held her hand out. "It's not my house, not my porch, but if you'd like to have a seat, you're more than welcome."

"Well, thank you. I will for a minute. It's been a busy day."

"Spring's like that. Everything kinda busts loose at once. Then you can't catch a breath until Thanksgiving rolls around."

"Ain't that the truth?" Mrs. Hudson smiled and nodded, the wisdom of age coloring her eyes and expression some, although she still had a youthful glow about her, and energy seemed to radiate off her. Along with kindness and love. Marlowe just hoped she grew to be that kind of woman.

"Definitely things got a lot busier at the feed store."

"Clark told me that you guys are together." Mrs. Hudson leaned over and patted Marlowe's hand. "It sure took you guys long enough. About the time you were in eighth grade, I kinda figured you guys would get together and nothing would ever split you up. You two just didn't see it."

"That's the truth. I didn't even one time consider the idea of Clark and me as anything other than best friends. It just seemed dangerous to mess with a friendship as good as ours."

"That's true. In all my years, I've seen very few people with the rapport that you two have. I've been hoping for this day for a really long time."

Marlowe looked off the porch as Kylie came running around the house, Gracie jumping along beside her. It was crazy the amount of fun a child could have with a dog. Gracie had a rope in her mouth, and Kylie carried the other end, and Marlowe wasn't sure whether they were playing tug-of-war, or they were just having fun carrying the rope between them.

"You seem a little pensive though. I thought you'd be really excited and happy. Is there something wrong?" Mrs. Hudson leaned in, then her lips formed an "O". "Is Dana giving you a hard time? She doesn't seem like she really likes anyone but herself, but I could see her being upset that Clark has moved on. She seemed to take a perverse kind of pleasure in seeing that he hadn't and maybe even thinking that he pined after her, in some weird egotistical way."

Marlowe had started to shake her head no, to answer Mrs. Hudson's first question. But then she ended up nodding along in agreement, because she could totally see what Mrs. Hudson was saying about Dana. It seemed a little like gossip, so she didn't add a comment of her own, other than, "Clark doesn't seem to notice it. At least if he has, he's never said anything to me about it bothering him."

"Me either. Though men usually don't talk about that stuff. Clark might with you. When you guys were growing up, and you'd hang out here in the kitchen, sometimes it would surprise me the things he'd say to you."

That definitely made her smile. It made her feel like she was special, even back in high school, to Clark.

"But I kind of veered off the subject of what I meant to be talking about. Are you okay?"

This time, Mrs. Hudson put her hand on Marlowe's and didn't move it. For some reason, that warm hand, and that kindly concern, made Marlowe's throat close and her eyes prick.

She wanted a mother so bad. Just someone to talk to about the decisions that she needed to make, the money she could have, what to do.

Before she knew it, the whole story had fallen out. About how she had given up what she wanted to raise Kylie. "And I don't regret it. I don't regret any of it. I would do it all over again in a heartbeat. Kylie's worth it. But I have this opportunity, and I feel like I should take it. Because I might never have it again."

"Which opportunity? The one with the money and your career, or the one with Clark?"

Marlowe paused. She had assumed the opportunity with Clark would still be there when she was finished with school. Wouldn't it?

"Are you suggesting I should give up the idea of going back to school?" She looked at Mrs. Hudson, really looked at her. The woman looked happy. She always did. Even when something bad was happening, like a few years ago when Loyal had gotten into the farm accident. Even in the hospital, Mrs. Hudson had a joy and peace that just radiated off her and also put everyone around her at peace.

"No. I didn't say that."

"Oh. Because I can't imagine anyone telling me that I shouldn't finish my education. I mean, I like working at the feed store, but it's not exactly the career I had planned for myself. And now, I have the opportunity to do more. To be more. Shouldn't I take that?"

Even as she asked the question, she really wasn't sure.

"More? More what? More educated? There is an opportunity for that, yes. But is that the only thing that matters?"

"No, of course not. Education doesn't make a person. But it does provide more opportunities. And it was my lifelong dream. It's what I always wanted. It was what was taken from me so brutally, along with the death of my mother and my sister."

"And that's what you still want?"

It was, wasn't it? Just because she hadn't thought about it in a while or longed for it maybe in a long time didn't mean her desire had faded. She still wanted that education that she hadn't been able to finish. Didn't she?

"I think that's what will make me happy."

"I think happiness is a choice."

"Yes. I suppose you're right about that."

"I would never tell you not to finish your education. But I guess I would tell you to pray about it. Because sometimes God shows us exactly what He wants for us and what truly will make us happy and is the best for us, and then he allows a temptation in our lives that might maybe distract us from making the best decision. It might be something that seems good or even practical. And a lot of times, it's definitely what the world would tell us to do.

"But I would turn my head away from everything the world says, because most of the time, what they say isn't what God wants for us."

That was a lot of words, and Marlowe took a moment to digest them. It was no shock to her that commonly accepted "wisdom," and social norms of the day, often ran directly contrary to what the Bible said. She'd known that.

But she'd never quite applied it to her life in this way before. Never thought about it in terms of her education before.

How much of her wanting to finish her degree was because that was really still what she wanted to do, and how much was it because she felt like that was what society thought she should do, if she had the opportunity? But there was something else that nagged at her. And Mrs. Hudson might have the answer.

"Do you think that Clark wouldn't wait for me?"

Mrs. Hudson's brows raised, and she tilted her head before her eyes met Marlowe's. "Do you think it's fair to ask him to?"

No. Of course it wasn't. She had to choose. Between two good things. She definitely wanted Clark more than she wanted any kind of college, but wasn't that stupid?

She heard all the time about women who regretted the decision of not having a career and found themselves depending on their husbands. It was just a downright ridiculously dumb choice for someone who had the opportunity to do something else.

Or was it?

"I can still be with Clark and finish my school as well. I could probably do most of it online." Even as she said that though, she knew it was impossible. She'd have to completely change her major. There were too many labs and other things that she'd have to complete.

Online learning would work for some. And she and Clark could probably work it out, but she wouldn't be focusing on the commitment that she made to him and their children; she'd be focusing on herself.

As she thought about it, it sounded selfish.

"There are so many women, so many stories about women who gave up a career or an education or opportunity for their husbands and families and regretted it. I don't want to give that up, I don't think, not because I want it so bad, but because I'm afraid I'll regret it. Can't I have it all?" She heard that all the time. Surely, she could.

"You probably can." Mrs. Hudson nodded. "Just like someone who wants to be a concert pianist could probably also play the tuba and the ukulele on a concert level as well, but they're probably better off focusing on one instrument."

"So you don't think it's a good idea?"

"I think only you can answer that question. My personal opinion, if you want it, is that you need to do what God wants you to do. And only you know what that is."

Chapter 16

Clark's stomach growled. Too bad, since he still had a hundred acres to plant before he could quit.

His mother had already spoken on the two-way, and she'd told him that she'd be stopping at his house to pick up Kylie. She thought Marlowe might bring his supper out.

But the car that was pulling along the edge of the road wasn't Marlowe's. It almost looked like Chandler's. Something low and fast and fancy.

Yeah, as the tractor got closer to the end of the field, Clark was pretty sure it was Chandler's car. There was no doubt it was when his brother got out, unfolding his long legs and towering over his squatting machine.

Clark turned the planter around at the end of the row and waited for his brother to stride over. He'd known Chandler would be in town shortly, because he was going to sell a month of his time at the auction and production on the movie he was making was just wrapping up.

But Chandler hadn't exactly specified when he was arriving, and Clark knew he'd be too busy with the spring work to be able to spend much time with him this time of year.

Nevertheless, he waited while his brother climbed up and opened the door of the tractor.

"You got room for a rider?" Chandler said, although he didn't wait for an answer, but stepped in and sat down on the dummy seat.

"For a little bit. Marlowe might be bringing my supper later though, and I figured she'd take a few turns with me."

"Yeah, it's been a few months since we've seen each other, and I've missed you too."

"Oh, stop it. You don't give a flip. You certainly don't expect me to miss you. And if you do, you don't have to leave."

"I can make more money in Hollywood than I can on this redneck farm, and for a lot less effort."

Clark figured it probably wasn't too much effort, since Chandler had always been a ham. Although, for Clark, he wouldn't want to have to do what Chandler had to do with some woman he didn't know and didn't care for. Maybe they used body doubles. Clark never asked. It wasn't something he really wanted to know, and it certainly wasn't anything that he would ever need to know.

"Everybody has their thing, I guess."

"Yeah."

Chandler's tone made Clark's head whip around. He'd always kind of seen Chandler as superficial and happy-go-lucky, but just in that one word, he thought he caught a glimpse of something a little deeper. A hurt.

"Anything you need to talk about?" Maybe he hadn't given Chandler as much thought as he should've. He just never seemed like the kind of guy that had any problems.

"Nah. Nothing to say."

Well, obviously he didn't want to talk about it. Clark sure as shooting wasn't going to pry, so he allowed the comment to pass and said, "What in the world possessed you to allow them to auction a month of your time?"

Chandler laughed and lifted a hand in innocence. "I don't think I really allowed it. Miss Lynette got my phone number from Mom, and she didn't really give me a chance to say no. I was agreeing before I realized I was."

Clark had to laugh at that. Miss Lynette could be very persuasive. And she was so organized it was almost like she had arguments for your backup, backup arguments.

"I guess I'm just a dirt-poor farmer and not a big, famous movie star. Because nobody asked me to donate a month of my time for the auction, thankfully."

Chandler snorted, but when he spoke, it was on a different subject. "Mom said you and Marlowe were together."

Wow. Word traveled fast. He knew it did in a small town, but Chandler was in L.A.

"Yeah." Clark was over the moon about it though, and he didn't mind talking about it. Actually, Marlowe was about the best subject he could think of that he'd like to talk about.

"You guys are such good friends, I think everybody could see it coming. Except, sometimes it seems like romance can ruin a friendship."

"Yeah, I was afraid of that. It seems like most couples have the passion and romance first, and then they kind of graduate to the friendship. I guess Marlowe and I did it backward. I think it's gonna work okay. She seems pretty smitten with me." He said the last a little sarcastically, and Chandler laughed like he expected him to.

"You were pretty lucky to have a friend like Marlowe growing up."

They'd come to the end of the road, and although his tractor wasn't ancient, it wasn't one of the newfangled ones that turned itself around using GPS, knowing exactly what shape the field was and where the obstacles were, right down to the telephone poles.

So it took a little more concentration, and Clark was glad of it. Because there was that note in Chandler's voice again. The note that he wasn't expecting from his easygoing brother.

"I know I was. God really blessed me with Marlowe."

"You guys spent so much time picking on and goofing off with each other, I'm not sure I can quite picture you guys romantically linked."

"I'm sure you'll get to see it. Watch closely, and let your big brother show you how it's done." More sarcasm, and Chandler laughed. It bothered Clark more than he wanted to say that something seemed to have shifted in Chandler's personality. It wasn't jadedness, necessarily. Clark guessed that it had something to do with L.A. and being gone from his hometown. Although Clark could be wrong. But that's how he'd feel if he had to leave his hometown. Like someone yanked the rug out from underneath him, and he'd be clawing to get back.

Chandler had never seemed to be a small-town kind of man.

They chatted some about the auction, and the tornado that had touched down in Trumbull, and even a little about Chandler's next film, and who might buy him at the auction as they went back and forth through the field a few more times.

Finally, they hit the end of the field again, and Chandler said, "I'm going to jump out here. I might as well run into town and see some folks. I don't think the auction's for two weeks, maybe I can find someone to take my place."

"Good luck with that. You're the only Hollywood movie star Cowboy Crossing has. I don't think anyone's going to take your place."

"You gotta face each day with optimism," Chandler said. "Otherwise, who could stand it?"

He jumped out of his seat, opened the door, and was down the steps while Clark was still thinking about his last words. They seemed kind of cryptic, which fit right in with the other things that seemed to be off with Chandler. Clark sure hoped he got them straightened out.

Or maybe less that he got them straightened out and more that he made sure that whatever he was doing was in line with what God wanted him to be doing. Clark knew how easy it was to get caught up in his own desires and what he wanted for his life, and he could move blithely right past what God had planned for him.

Take Dana, for example. It wasn't saying the divorce was okay, because once he was married, he would have stayed married, no matter how miserable he was, if it had been up to him. But it was more the idea he was with her to begin with. Looking back at his experience with Dana, he could see he was totally doing what he wanted, and he hadn't cared what God wanted.

Marlowe, on the other hand, seemed to be exactly what God wanted him to have.

He figured he'd better be careful, though, because he wanted Marlowe, and he needed to make sure he wasn't rushing ahead and taking something God didn't have planned for him. Even though things were working out, as only God could work them out.

He'd only made one pass down and back up the long field when he saw that Marlowe was parked where Chandler had been.

He turned around and was getting ready to stop and go get her, or at least talk to her, when she walked over. Still, he had time to hop out of the tractor and greet her on the ground.

It was kinda new, this idea that he could greet Marlowe with a kiss. New, and very nice in a pleasant way.

She seemed to think so too. She smiled at him and came closer, not stopping. He wrapped his arms around her and lowered his head. She reached out, the bag she held bumping against his back as she put her arms around his shoulders and pressed into him.

Yeah, there was definitely something to be said about falling in love with and kissing his best friend.

He lifted his head just slightly. Falling in love? That's what had happened, wasn't it? He looked at her with a little bit of wonder in his eyes, and she looked back, a little confusion in hers, almost wonder, like she was trying to figure out what in the world he was thinking.

He could tell her; he could always tell her anything. Marlowe had always respected him and how he felt.

"What?"

"I think I've fallen in love with you. I think that's what this is."

Her lips pressed together, although they still turned up, and her eyes held humor. "Really? You're just now figuring that out?" She shook her head. "I love you. I've always loved you as a friend. But it's pretty obvious that I'm in love with you now."

"I said it first."

"Nope. Pretty sure I did. You were questioning whether or not you were falling in love with me. I flat-out told you I love you." Her brows lifted in challenge.

"Okay. To prove that I love you, I'll let you win. Because that's what love does, it lets the other person win."

She twisted her tongue, biting it and closing one eye. "That's your convoluted way of trying to get me to tell you that you won, isn't it?" She nodded knowingly. "I'm totally not falling for that."

He shrugged a shoulder. "It's up to you. I'm just saying real love doesn't have to be first."

"Okay. I'm down for that. I'll ride with you in the tractor, and I'll be second into the cab."

He laughed, and she joined in.

"Come on, if you're gonna ride with me, I'll help you up. You can go first."

They didn't really say too much until they were both in the tractor and he'd started out across the field. He'd gotten the container with the casserole she'd brought situated in his lap, with one hand on the steering wheel and one hand holding his fork. "You know, normally when someone brings food out to someone who's working in the field, it's a sandwich or finger food."

"Are you complaining?" She pursed her lips, but he knew she was joking.

"Yeah. This is stinking hard."

"I'm sorry." Her voice was sincere. "I wasn't expecting to bring you supper. Then Dana came for Huck, and your mom came and took Kylie, and I ended up bringing you food." She shrugged her shoulders. "I had to bring you what I had."

"I know. I'm just teasing you. It's really good. I don't know what it is, but you can make this any time you want, and I will help you eat it all."

"I'll write that down in my little black book."

"I don't think that's what the little black book is for. Actually, I think the little black book thing is outdated. People keep information like that on their phones nowadays."

"I guess you're right. Sorry. I'm old-fashioned. Is that going to be a problem?"

"Going to be? It hasn't been, has it?"

There was a pause. Bigger than a normal pause, and it made him turn and look at her.

"I guess not. I just didn't know how things are going to change." She looked down and kind of played with the seam of her jeans for a little bit. "The insurance adjuster offered me a check. They're going to completely total the house. Although I can choose to not have it replaced, since there's no mortgage on it. The money could be mine."

"It's yours, and you can do what you want with it." He wasn't sure what she was saying, although she seemed to be gauging his response. Did she think that he expected her to give it to him? "We're not old-fashioned that way, are we?"

"What way?"

"I don't know. You just seem like you're expecting me to say something, and I'm not sure exactly what you're expecting."

"Nothing about being old-fashioned, I guess. Actually, it's more of a modern thing. I would have money to take Kylie and go to St. Louis and finish my degree."

If she lifted her fist and punched him in the stomach, he wasn't sure he'd have been more surprised.

"Is St. Louis the only place you can do that?" Was she seriously going to leave? What about their relationship? What was she thinking about that?

In a way, it felt like Dana all over again. Although Dana had gone to New York City, which was, of course, slightly further than St. Louis.

At least, Marlowe wasn't thinking of leaving Missouri. He couldn't imagine living anywhere else. He was proud of the rich history, their status as the gateway to the west, the reputation of being tough and resilient and taking whatever the weather threw at them.

He couldn't think about leaving it.

On a smaller scale, though, he supposed he could imagine leaving the farm. Maybe. Although he came from generations of farmers and had always been proud of it.

Sure, when they were younger, Marlowe talked all the time about chemistry and how much she loved it and how much she wanted to get her degree in it. But in the same breath, she'd said there were no jobs for chemistry majors around here. She'd have to get another degree, and even then, jobs were scarce, even if one lived in the city. But maybe that's what she was thinking.

Suddenly, the chicken casserole that he was eating tasted like Styrofoam. He set the fork down and handed the container to Marlowe before he reached the end of the row and turned the tractor and planter around.

"Nooo," she drew the word out, finally answering his question. "Of course not. There are colleges all over the country where I could go. I just thought St. Louis was the best for me and Kylie. Not too far, but big enough to be what we need."

"Well, if it's the best for Kylie and you, then that's where you should go." He knew that with all his heart.

The heart that all of a sudden hurt with every slow beat.

Hadn't he just been thinking maybe he was pushing things too hard? And about how he had rushed into things with Dana, and done exactly what he wanted, and hadn't waited on God to make it clear exactly what he should do?

Maybe this was another one of those things that he just wanted so bad he couldn't see that God was saying no.

He didn't want that to be true though. He wanted Marlowe. He loved her, and they were so perfect together.

He wanted to argue with the Lord right away, but he didn't want Marlowe to be privy to that argument, which, he suspected, would be more like begging.

"Just like that?" Her voice held tones of surprise.

"Yeah." That was the only word he could get out of his tight throat. The burning on the inside of his chest wanted to erupt out of his mouth. His heart and soul wanted to beg her to change her mind, to stay. But the smaller, rational part of him said it couldn't be his decision, and it wasn't right of him to try to guilt her into anything.

"So you're okay with that?"

He couldn't stop the tractor, but he did look over at her. "I'm okay with whatever is best for you and for Kylie. Even if it's not what I want."

She rubbed the tips of her fingers together and said slowly, "You could come too."

Could he? Could he leave the farm? What would he do?

But he knew there were plenty of jobs for a guy like him. He knew lots of kids who'd grown up on Missouri family farms that had gone bankrupt or sold out and been taken over by larger farms.

It wasn't anything new since it seemed like a person needed more and more ground to be able to make a living on a farm anymore.

So far, he and his brothers had been able to manage by keeping his expenses low, hence the older tractor.

Lots of kids he'd gone to school with were now salesmen, used cars or farm equipment big and small. He knew several who worked as repairmen, and he'd done enough fixing of his own that he would probably be qualified to work on somebody else's stuff, or it wouldn't be hard to learn.

Yeah, he could do it. He could leave the farm.

"Is that what you want from me?" He felt like it would change a fundamental part of himself.

He was a farmer. A Missouri farmer, which meant he was tough and resilient, and he could get knocked down, and he could—no, would—keep getting up. But if she wanted him to be something else...do something else, which would make him be something else, yeah, he thought he could.

If it meant they'd be together, he'd do it.

"I can't ask you to change who you are."

"I appreciate that."

"But I don't think I can give this up. I'll never have the opportunity again. It's completely unexpected that this second chance even came up. I have to follow where it leads, wherever that is." She waved her arm around, indicating all the area outside. "I mean, I guess I could be giving up what's between us, but I don't even know what that is, exactly, or where it might be going." Her face was pinched, like the thought was painful.

He didn't know how to make it easier. It was hard on him, too. His heart felt old and wrinkled. Used.

He spoke. "You can say marriage. If this," he waved his arms between them, "leads to marriage. Because that's where these things often do lead. And I certainly wouldn't enter into a relationship with any other ideas in my mind. I assumed you wouldn't either."

"You're right. Marriage. If this leads to marriage, then I'll be here for the rest of my life, and I'll never have the opportunity to finish my degree, and go on, and make my way in the world, like I'd wanted to in school."

He nodded. "I get it. I know how hard it was for you to leave college and come back and take Kylie. I know it's a big sacrifice. For a while, there was a lot of grief from losing your mom and sister, but the idea was always there, this wasn't what you'd asked for, and it wasn't what you wanted. I guess I just kind of developed the idea over time, because you never seem to be upset or angry or bitter, and it seemed like you'd grown to love this life."

Wishful thinking on his part, apparently.

She was a clerk at the feed store. He supposed there were a lot of people who would say that didn't amount to much and that she could have been a lot more, could be a lot more still.

"I thought you'd understand. I wasn't really expecting you to be overly thrilled about it. And I know the timing is bad. But I didn't choose the storm or the tree. We both know that was the Lord working things out. He put this opportunity here, the opportunity for me to finish school, and He even provided the money." She shook her head and looked out the tractor window at the field that he'd almost finished planting. Straight rows. And true. Year after year, the same. He understood that was boring for a lot of people. He hadn't thought Marlowe was one of them.

"I just think this might be what God wants me to do." She shrugged her shoulders and looked at him.

"I get it." He looked back out the windshield at the same field. How many times had he planted? Years, decades. Seasons turned, the years flew by, and he was still here, working the ground. Like his ancestors before him. He knew, without a doubt, that this was where God wanted him.

"As a man, I want to go with you." He knew he could make a living off the farm, and he wanted more than anything to be with Marlowe. "But I'm positive God wants me to stay here."

"That's what I figured."

They were quiet for a while, and he went back and forth in the field a few times. She'd ridden with him plenty through the years. This was nothing new. There was more conversation, exchanging some information about Huck and Kylie and their schedules, but it was strained and without the humor and banter that usually marked their interactions.

For the first time ever, it was almost a relief when she got out of the tractor. Not that he wanted to see her go, just that it was so painful to be with her, knowing that he'd declared his love for her, and her for him, and yet she was still going to leave.

Chapter 17

When Marlowe stepped down from the tractor, her heart felt like it weighed more than a bucket of sand, and she wished that there was something she could do to restore the natural comradery that had always been so easy between Clark and her.

But she supposed this was to be expected, since of course he wasn't going to be happy with her leaving. The timing was awful as well.

But it wasn't really her timing, right?

She only wished she was as sure as he was about the Lord's will for her life. It wasn't something that she'd ever questioned too much.

College had seemed a natural choice. Then when Kylie needed a mom, that seemed pretty straightforward too. Maybe she just had it too easy in her life. Not that her life had been easy, but it'd been easy to see God's will. This seemed a little bit more blurry and less black-and-white.

She had something to drop off for Miss Lynette, which was good, since she didn't feel like staying in for the night anyway, even though it was almost dark. So she grabbed the auction items from Clark's house and then drove on into town.

Arriving at the church, she saw there were lights on in the basement.

Lynette was probably working overtime to get everything ready, and Marlowe was happy she could help.

"Oh, Marlowe, I'm so glad you were able to bring that over tonight," Lynette said as Marlowe opened the basement door and stepped in.

Marlowe held out her items. "You're here working awfully late on this."

"Not really. I'm almost done. But I had to school the children, and then I had several hospital visits I wanted to do, and I also had to get the Sunday School lesson ready and some baked goods to take to shut-ins. I just wanted to squeeze this in before I quit for the day."

Marlowe had no idea where Lynette found all of her energy, but she managed to do the work of about seven people.

After raising Kylie for the last five years, Marlowe couldn't imagine having eight children. One was enough to wear her to a frazzle.

"Mrs. Hudson was around, and she said that you and Clark were together." Lynette clapped her hands, her face smiling in excitement, "I just always thought you two would make the most wonderful couple. I'm so excited for you."

"Yeah. Thanks."

Lynette's face went from smiling and animated to lowered brows, and she put a hand on Marlowe's arm. "What's wrong? You don't sound like a woman in love."

Marlowe hadn't planned on saying anything, but there was just something about Lynette that encouraged her to confide, and she spilled everything. It was a good twenty minutes later when she threw up her hands and said, "I just don't know what to do. I love Clark, and I want to be with him more than anything. But I just can't give up this opportunity. It's crazy to not finish my education and get a good job like I know I can do. I used to be considered kind of intelligent, back in the day." Life had a way of making her forget she used to be considered someone with potential.

"Yeah, kids bring you down to the basics, don't they?" Lynette said almost dryly.

Marlowe figured if anybody understood, Lynette would. Maybe once upon a time, Lynette had dreams of her own too, but now everything she did was wrapped up in her children and her husband.

Marlowe looked at her with new eyes. "Doesn't that bother you? That your whole life is other people?"

If Lynette had looked surprised, or if she had acted like *of course my life is other people, isn't that the way it's supposed to be?*, Marlowe might have had a harder time accepting her answer. But when Lynette looked at her, it was through eyes of understanding.

"It's hard to swim against the current, isn't it?"

That wasn't exactly what Marlowe had been expecting her to say, and her forehead wrinkled. "What do you mean?"

"A hundred years ago, we wouldn't even be having this discussion, would we? But now, it's accepted, as a social fact, that a woman is weak if she doesn't have her own life and her own career and her own job and her own everything." Lynette's eyes held compassion, and maybe a little bit of hesitation, as though she knew her words weren't ones that were popular. "I guess, when I look in the Bible, I don't see that."

"But the Proverbs thirty-one woman. She was a businesswoman, and she worked. She did all kinds of things on her own. That's all Bible." Marlowe had heard that teaching over and over growing up.

Lynette sighed. "I think we might take that a little bit too far. Because it's pretty clear in Scripture that the Proverbs thirty-one woman was a wife and mother first. She did those other things, true. But her main interest, always and forever, was for her husband and her family. She wasn't doing those things to have a career of her own. Was she?"

Marlowe shook her head slowly, thinking about the passage in her head. She didn't have to think long. Lynette was right. A lot of times, it was easy to take the Bible and twist it to make it say what she wanted it to say, and mean what she wanted it to mean, rather than what it actually said.

"And it's as clear as day in all of the passages in the New Testament regarding wives and mothers. There is nowhere that suggests even remotely that what we do in our society today is what should be done."

Marlowe nodded. She already knew that. Which was why she always thought of the Proverbs thirty-one woman, because there were no other passages to back her up.

"You should always look to Scripture, but God has a plan for your life. It might not be what you want, what you think is best for you, but

God certainly isn't going to ask you to do anything that would harm you or not be best for you."

"So I was thinking that you thought I should be with Clark, but now I'm not so sure. What do you think? What should I choose?"

Lynette smiled. A small, sweet smile. "Choose God's will." She lifted her hand a little.

"I was afraid you were going to say that. What do you think God's will is?"

"He's only going to show it to you. He's certainly not going to tell me what you should do with your life."

"I'm asking your advice. If you were me, and outside of whether or not either one is God's will, which do you recommend that I do?"

"Does Clark want you to go and get your degree and move to the city?"

"He doesn't care. I mean of course he doesn't want me to go. But he's okay with it."

"Does he love you anyway?"

"Hmmm?"

"Does he need you to have a degree in order for you to be worthy of his love? Does he need you to be different than what you are?"

"Of course not. He loves me just like I am. But that's not really answering the question. I know he loves me. I just don't know if I should go or if I should stay."

"I think," Lynette said thoughtfully, "I think the confusion comes because what society expects of us is so loud and clear. And also the cases, where a man doesn't take care of his wife, and she ends up regretting not having a job or an education, are so heartbreaking and newsworthy. But for every case like that, there are thousands more, ten thousand more, where that doesn't happen and where the woman is satisfied and at peace, and blissfully happy, because she knows that she chose what really mattered. A career is fleeting. It doesn't last. You can't take it to heaven with you. Your family? It's eternal. And I think the devil has us deluded. It's just one more way he uses to rip families apart. Because when there's no stable mother, there's no stable anchor in the home. And that's what those verses, Proverbs thirty-one, and all the New Testament verses on wives and mothers, are for. The husbands have a place, they provide. The wives have a place, they nurture and keep the home. It's your kingdom."

Marlowe could see that. After all, when she had the choice about whether or not to take Kylie, she hadn't even needed two seconds to think about it. Because Kylie was a person, her niece, and she knew what she needed to do. People were more important—her niece was more important—than any kind of degree or education. She'd known that.

"But again," Lynette said. "I'd make sure that what you choose lines up with what you know the Lord wants for you."

Marlowe nodded, pretty sure she understood what Lynette was saying. And knowing that Lynette would only give her advice that lined up with what the Bible said.

They chatted for a bit more before Marlowe left.

Chapter 18

Saturday morning, it was raining, and Clark was in the kitchen when Marlowe came down. The smell of bacon wafted in the air, and her stomach rumbled.

"Morning, sleepyhead." Clark turned around and greeted her, but she didn't think it was her imagination that his smile didn't reach his eyes. He wasn't very happy with their conversation yesterday in the tractor, and she couldn't blame him.

She'd tossed and turned all night too. It wasn't like she had forever to make up her mind. She needed to make a decision. She couldn't expect Clark to wait forever.

Huck hadn't even entered into the conversation. But he should be considered as well. Although she knew, with certainty, that if her marrying Clark would help Huck in any way, she'd do it in a heartbeat.

"Aren't the kids up yet?" she asked.

"They're up, and I told them they could go outside until breakfast was ready." He grabbed the plate that was sitting on the counter and held it by the skillet. "Which it is. Would you mind running out and telling them to come on in?"

"Sure." She hoped her word came out in a happy tone. Because she felt anything but. She knew she'd brought it on herself, but he hadn't greeted her with a smile or a kiss, and their normal banter was completely gone. It was no less than what she deserved. But it still made her heart ache.

Five minutes later, the kids were sitting at the table, their hands and faces washed and breakfast steaming on plates in front of them. Clark sat at the head, and she sat on his right. She hadn't had a mom and a dad growing up in her home, so she wasn't sure how normal families did it, but she hadn't wanted to sit at the other end of the table, with the whole thing between Clark and her. She wanted to sit beside him.

She liked the picture that made better, not that she wanted him to make all of her decisions for her or anything, nothing like that. She was still her own person. But she liked the idea of walking beside someone.

How many times growing up had she wished she had a father?

Wasn't that what made a family?

And here she provided for two small children, and yet she was thinking about giving that up, taking that away from them, and doing what she thought would make her happy. But deep down, although she'd be hard-pressed to find very many people who agreed with her, she didn't think she would be more satisfied or happy on her own.

Not only would her heart be aching to be separated from Clark, but she just didn't think—no, she knew—God hadn't made her, nor him, to walk alone.

That was the clarity she'd been missing last night. But she still wasn't entirely sure, so she let the chatter of the children go on uninterrupted, and she didn't say anything. Not yet. But she did feel she was one step closer to making the right decision.

She started listening again, just in time to hear Huck telling Clark about what he had done with Dana last night.

Clark was listening so intently he didn't even correct his son for talking with his mouth full.

Huck swallowed. "She had some man there, and they wanted me to do a bunch of stuff. And the man didn't look very happy."

"He didn't? Why not?" Clark paused with his fork midair, and Marlowe wasn't even sure he knew it.

Huck shrugged his shoulders, typical unconcern. "I don't know. It was fun, at first, because they let me play with trucks. But then they brought Molly in. And they told me I had to play with her, and I didn't want to because she wanted to play dolls, and she's not like Kylie. She was mean. And then they wanted me to hold her hand. But I didn't want to get any closer to her. She didn't smell good. That's when the man wasn't happy."

"And your mom wanted you to do this?" Clark's voice had gotten softer.

Marlowe didn't hear that tone out of him very often, but she knew exactly what it meant. Dana was in big trouble. She would've smiled if she hadn't been so outraged herself. What had that woman been doing with Huck?

"Yeah. She told me to do whatever the man said. And I tried to, because you told me that I always have to obey adults. But I don't want to do that again." Huck got a mulish look on his face, and Marlowe almost smiled, because he looked just like his dad. "And they didn't let me eat until it was over, and it lasted a really long time."

"But you did get something to eat eventually, correct?" Clark said, and the threatening note was almost gone from his voice, although it was still soft.

"Yeah. They gave me a doughnut." Huck shoved another forkful of egg in his mouth, and he looked across the table at Kylie. "Are we still going to race our bikes after breakfast?"

The two kids chatted, and Clark's eyes lifted and met Marlowe's.

"I guess it's no longer a mystery as to why she wants custody. It sounds like she either has a part for him to play already, or she's trying to push him into it."

Marlowe's heart hurt, but she nodded, feeling bad for Clark, because he didn't need this kind of complication in his life. He would never let Dana get away with it.

"It almost makes it better. We kind of knew there was something going on, and this makes everything clear."

His cell phone rang, and it showed how distracted he was, because he answered it while still sitting at the table, and she'd never known a time she'd eaten with him that she'd ever seen him on his cell phone at the table.

She only listened to his conversation with half an ear, because Kylie asked her if she and Huck could fly kites, and then they started talking about where the kites were. She got involved in that, but she could tell Clark's conversation was something serious by the look on his face.

Clark slid his phone off and smiled at her, a real smile. It had to have been good news.

"What?" she asked.

His smile got bigger. "That was Judge Rhodes. Apparently, Dana and Cody ate at the diner this morning on their way out of town, and they discussed what was apparently an audition for Huck over breakfast. They happened to be in the booth behind Judge Rhodes." His smile almost turned into a smirk as he set his phone down on the table. "Mr. Rhodes wasn't impressed when Dana started talking about the audition and how she'd been filing for custody so she could make money from Huck." His tone lowered. "But I'm pretty sure she sealed her fate when she called her kid a brat." His eyes cut to Huck, who was deep in conversation with Kylie about the best way to get a kite in the air.

"I honestly can't even believe she would say that, even knowing Dana."

Clark nodded.

"Wasn't Judge Rhodes the man that you worked for all through high school? On the pig farm west of town?"

"Yes. I came on and gave them a hand along with his hired guys when he went on vacation every September. And March." His hand touched his fork, but he didn't pick it up. "That could've been a lot different, and the Lord really worked that out perfectly. Judge Rhodes might not have my custody case, but not all cases are decided in the courtroom."

Marlowe nodded. There was a lot of finagling that went on; even with her limited experience, she knew that much.

"I'm happy for you, and I'm very relieved for Huck."

"Monday, I might have to make some phone calls, but I'm pretty sure we can get this straightened out. She might not even be allowed to visit anymore, if what Judge Rhodes was saying works out. She obviously doesn't have Huck's best interests at heart."

"Not a surprise to us, although it is kind of shocking that a mother could act like that."

"After Monday, I don't think we'll have to worry too much about Dana." Clark looked at his fingers, but he probably wasn't seeing the fork in his hand. He lifted his gaze. "I guess what I'm saying is we had talked about needing to be married, but I don't think that's gonna be necessary after all. I know you are willing to do it, and I appreciate that." His chest rose and fell. "It looks like the Lord might've worked that out for us too. For you. If you're still wondering whether or not you should go, that's not holding you back anymore."

"I guess it's good to know." She wasn't sure that would make a difference. She'd already pretty much made up her mind. She thought anyway.

It was something she should probably tell him, but suddenly she realized it was getting late. "Oh my goodness, I need to get going. With the feed store's extended hours, we're open until one o'clock on Saturdays, and it's my day to work. I need to get in there." She pushed back away from the table as Clark nodded. He'd known she was working and already planned on watching Kylie. She had let time slip away from her.

She was still fifteen minutes early when she pulled into the feed store. Definitely tonight she and Clark needed to talk. She wasn't one hundred percent sure on her decision, but she needed to be by this evening. It wasn't fair to string Clark along. He'd been supportive and sweet, and she was taking advantage of him.

They had a rush of customers when they opened at eight, and Marlowe didn't think too much more about it until things slowed down around ten.

That's when the Cromwells came in. Mrs. Cromwell held the baby in one hand while pushing the cart that held the two other children in it, with the oldest walking beside her. They followed her husband around the store.

The older children were well-behaved, but the baby was fussy.

Finally, Mr. Cromwell turned around and said loud enough for the entire store to hear, although they were the only customers, "If you can't get the kid to shut up, take it outside."

Mrs. Cromwell smiled, a little sad in Marlowe's opinion, and with a long-suffering look on her face, she lifted the two children out of the cart, and they all followed her out the door.

Mr. Cromwell turned. "Adam, get back here. You push the cart."

The oldest son looked up at his mother, and she nodded.

Adam returned to his dad and put his hands on the cart.

Marlowe turned away. Mr. Long stood at the end of the counter, watching as well. When Marlowe moved back around, his eyes went to hers.

She didn't figure he'd say anything about the Cromwells, and neither did she.

"Everything going okay this morning?" Mr. Long asked.

She was kind of surprised he was in; it was Saturday, after all. She nodded. "It was really busy when we opened this morning, but things slowed down."

He nodded. "That's a Saturday for you." He tapped on the counter with his fingers, his eyes kinda staring off into the distance.

It was unlike Mr. Long, and Marlowe moved closer, putting her hand on his. "Is everything okay?"

"Yeah. Well, the missus isn't doing so great. I've been thinking about retiring."

Marlowe almost smiled. Mr. Long thought about retiring a lot. Although this was the first that he'd mentioned his wife's health.

"I don't think the store would run without you," she said. "I say Mrs. Long needs to get better, because I think she knows that too. We need you."

"I want to be here. Although Mrs. Long would like to do some traveling, and I've kinda got a hankering to spend a little more time with her than I have been. I guess her sickness isn't bad, but it's made me think. We don't have a lot of time left. And I'm happiest when I'm with her. As much as I love the store, and everything we do here, and Mrs. Long has always supported me, I just knew she missed me when I wasn't there, and maybe it's time for us to do a few things together."

Mr. Long never talked like that, and Marlowe's stomach dipped and swayed at the thought of the man who was almost like a father to her not being there anymore. It would be really odd working for someone other than Mr. Long. Of course, she'd get used to it, but still, change was hard, especially when one was looking at losing someone one admired and trusted as much as she did Mr. Long.

But there was no point in borrowing trouble, so she didn't. "I think that's a smart idea. I'm sure Mrs. Long will be pretty happy if she hears you're going to be home."

Mr. Long chuckled. "I'll have a honey do list about a mile and half long."

"I bet you could talk her into doing it with you."

Mr. Cromwell and Adam came to the counter then, and Marlowe checked them out. Mrs. Cromwell never came back in. Marlowe didn't blame her.

She didn't know what the Lord was trying to tell her with this, although she kind of felt like maybe He was saying something. Mr. Long and Mrs. Long's marriage which had spanned decades and was happy versus the Cromwells' marriage where Mr. Cromwell was a jerk and Mrs. Cromwell was a saint.

There. Maybe that was it. The world would tell Marlowe that she needed that degree and that career, even though she wasn't sure she wanted it anymore, in fact was certain that she didn't. But she needed it for back up, just in case she ended up married to someone like Mr. Cromwell.

She would have a marriage like the Longs with Clark. Because he was about the opposite of Mr. Cromwell. She wouldn't have to daily take up a cross and die to herself in order to stay married to her husband. Being married to Clark would be fun. She could almost bet that would be true every day.

She'd always kind of felt like God messed up her life when he'd allowed her mother and sister and her husband to be killed and, while she hadn't minded stepping up and adopting Kylie, she'd not seen it as God's best for her.

Now, it was hard to believe that she would have been happier away from Cowboy Crossing and Kylie and Clark.

In fact, she knew she wouldn't have been.

She grunted as the realization swept over her – God had been working everything out for years, and she'd been too busy being bitter at Him and hadn't taken the time to see that what He'd given her was better than what she'd wanted.

With those thoughts, peace settled in her chest, and she felt lighter and cool, and a weight she hadn't even realized she'd been carrying around floated away until it was gone. She couldn't wait to talk to Clark.

Chapter 19

Marlowe ended up doing inventory and restocking shelves with Mr. Long after the feed store closed at one. It wasn't something she normally did, but since they were shorthanded, and since it was the busy time of year, she put the hours in.

They worked quickly, though, since Clark had texted her around two saying that a bad line of storms might be coming through before supper.

Mr. Long had left, and Marlowe was just finishing up when Clark's dad, who owned the store, stopped in.

"It's looking good in here," he said as he came around the end of the aisle where Marlowe had organized the rakes, shovels, and pitchforks.

She looked up, surprised at the sound of his voice. She put a hand to her heart. "I didn't hear you come in."

"Sorry. I used my key and came in the back."

Her heart still thudded, but she thought she sounded calm. "I'm glad you like what we did. We put some items we thought might be impulse buys at the end of the aisle. Those kids' gloves are just adorable. I actually bought a pair for both Kylie and Huck."

Mr. Hudson smiled, looking so much like Clark that Marlowe had to stare. This was probably how Clark would look in twenty-five years.

"It looks like you're almost done, and I don't want to keep you because of the weather. I do appreciate you staying. You've been doing a lot of things that aren't your job lately."

"I enjoy it, but I really enjoy having customers come in and enjoy shopping here." It was the truth. Of course, she enjoyed being home, but she also liked looking for ways to make the feed store better.

"That's one of the things I like about you." Mr. Hudson shifted and looked at the shelf above her head, as though gathering his thoughts. "That's not really why I'm here. I suppose you've been hearing from Mr. Long that he's thinking about retiring."

"He did mention that today," Marlowe said, scooping up the cardboard pieces she'd left on the floor and straightening. "But he's said that before."

"I think he's serious this time. He and his wife have plans for a cruise."

"Yeah, we talked about that this afternoon while we were working." She grinned. "I think he's pretty excited."

"I want you to take his place."

"While he's gone? Sure. I can do it." It was only a ten-day cruise. She could handle the store for that long.

"Then, yes. But I want him to train you to take his place. I want you to manage the store when he retires."

She stood with her mouth opened, shocked. She hadn't expected this. It was on the tip of her tongue to argue—she didn't have any kind of business degree or experience—but neither did Mr. Long. He'd just learned on the job and done the best he could. How many times had he said that over the years?

Marlowe thought about God's timing and plan. He'd opened the door for her education... She still loved chemistry and probably always would, but also loved her job at the feed store and life in a small town. An online business degree was doable, and God had just opened this door. She could have what she wanted most—Clark and a family—and also what she wanted next—to finish her education. It just wouldn't look quite like what she had thought it would.

"You think about it." Mr. Hudson shifted. "In the meantime, I definitely think you ought to be getting home. These storms might not amount to much, but I'd feel better knowing you are at home with Clark."

"Thank you, Mr. Hudson," she said. Her answer was almost a sure yes, but she wanted to talk to Clark about it. He'd almost certainly be happy for her and okay with it, but she wanted to make sure.

Despite the darkening sky, her heart was light on the way home. But by the time she pulled in, it was hard to pull her eyes away from the gray-green color in the western sky.

Clark stood on the porch, waiting. He'd texted while she was driving home, but she hadn't stopped to answer him.

His lips smiled, despite his pinched face, when she pulled in.

"I was about ready to come after you. Dad said you left fifteen minutes ago." Clark was at her door before she came to a complete stop.

She felt bad about the worry lines on his forehead that were her fault. "I'm sorry. I didn't want to stop and answer you on the way home."

"It's okay. I'd rather you be safe." He put his arms around her as soon as she stood up. "I sent the kids down to the cellar with blankets already. I told them they could play games on the iPad." He squinted at the sky. "I think we have about ten minutes." He brushed her hair back and pulled her closer. "Man, you had me worried."

"I'm sorry. I should have texted you before I left, but I was talking to your dad and thinking about some things."

"Oh?"

"Have you talked to him?"

"Crops and stuff. Not about you, but I'm sure Mom told him about us. Or..." His voice trailed off like he wasn't sure what to call them. He still thought she was leaving.

"He talked to me about managing the feed store since Mr. Long is retiring. I thought maybe you said something to him."

A gust of wind whipped across the yard. He waited for it to pass. "No. I didn't know about Mr. Long. He's really doing it this time?"

"That's what your dad said."

"Dad wants you to take his place?" He smiled, but then his face fell. "Did you tell him you were leaving?"

"No."

"You probably should." His face seemed guarded, like he was trying hard to be supportive of her and not give her any guilt because her choice wasn't what he wanted. She appreciated it.

"I'm staying," she blurted out.

He paused, then shook his head. "No. I don't want you to give up your opportunity. Not for me. Not for anything."

"I'm going to manage the feed store. I want to get a business degree, and I can do that online. But I wanted to talk to you first."

"Oh."

She was pretty sure he was stunned, but in a happy kind of way. She swallowed. She hadn't planned this next thing, but it felt like the right thing to do.

Pulling back a little, she took one of his loosened hands and dropped to one knee. Her stomach knotted, and her throat felt like parched earth, but she opened her mouth. "Clark, you've been my best friend forever. You know I love you, and we're even living together. I was kind of hoping you'd make an honest woman of me... I don't have a ring, but would you marry me?"

"You're not supposed to have a ring. Holy smokes, woman, I'm not wearing a diamond on my finger."

She shrugged. "That's what they always say in the movies. I couldn't come up with anything else. It was a little spur-of-the-moment." She sighed. "It's uncomfortable down here, and there's a storm coming, in case you forgot. Would you please answer me instead of complaining I didn't do it right?"

"It should only happen once. You need to do it well."

"I didn't see you jumping on the opportunity. Someone had to."

"Seriously, Low Beam? You told me you were leaving. I couldn't ask you when you weren't staying."

"You're stalling, Gable."

"Yep. You look good down there. In fact, I think you ought to kneel at my feet more often."

That was it. She started to push to her feet.

He dropped to his knees. "Kidding. I, honestly, was a little miffed you beat me to it."

"I can stand up and let you have at it."

"I don't have a ring."

"I already said that."

"Okay, then."

She straightened, her heart light and happy that they were back to normal.

"Will you marry me?" Clark said, his face completely serious.

"I will," she said, not even bothering to try to not sound smug. "I must point out that I asked first *and* answered first."

He stood, his dimple popping and his head lowering. "That's fine. Because I'm kissing you first."

Epilogue

Chandler sat in his parent's front yard, controlled chaos going on all around him, and tried to look happy.

His mother was only too excited to throw an impromptu engagement party for Clark and Marlowe when they'd announced that they planned to get married, and all five of her boys were here.

The yard rang with laughter and children playing, his brothers bantering and goofing off. It probably wouldn't be long before they'd set up targets and have a shooting contest. He could hold his own with any of it.

But he'd been fighting this restless, irritable feeling for a while.

It was the only thing he could think of that had made him agree to give one whole month of his time to be auctioned off next week.

What had he been thinking?

He didn't want to be at someone's beck and call for a month. He'd thought Miss Lynette was going to reach through the phone and hug the tar out of him when he'd agreed.

Really, he could back out, but that would only confirm everyone's opinion of him that he never followed through or did anything hard.

His family didn't consider making movies hard. And he couldn't really argue with them, because even the worst day on the movie set was a walk in the park compared to most of the workdays his brothers put in.

Plus, he couldn't explain it, but he wasn't happy in Hollywood anymore.

Maybe because he'd become too much like everyone else there, with one failed marriage behind him and a daughter that he hardly ever saw. Life sucked sometimes. And he didn't get do-overs.

Something told him, if he didn't change course, he'd be making more and bigger mistakes and would be looking at himself in ten years wishing for more than one do-over.

What better way to get away from himself and his potential for mistakes than to get back to his childhood teaching of leaving things in God's hands?

If auctioning himself off to the highest bidder wasn't allowing God to have control, he didn't know what was.

Hopefully, God wouldn't let any of his brothers buy him, since they'd put him to work from sunup until sundown on the farm.

Actually, he didn't mind farm work, but he'd always wanted to do it a little differently than what his family had.

Maybe, once this auction thing was over, and he'd fulfilled his obligations for his next movie, he'd buy a little spread and see if he couldn't get his ex to give him some more time with his daughter. He thought maybe that's what he needed. Or wanted.

No more wives, though. One broken marriage was enough.

"Okay, everyone, we're going to cut the cake now." His mom stood at the picnic table, a big knife clasped in her work-roughened hand. His parents might own a big mansion on the hill, but his mother still did all the yardwork and gardening herself.

Chandler smiled good-naturedly as Deacon slapped him on the back, passing him as his daughter, Tinsley, dragged him quickly toward the cake.

Clark stood beside their mother, his arm around his childhood friend and now fiancée, a huge, happy grin on his face.

"I can't believe it took them this long to figure out they were perfect for each other," Zane said, coming up beside Chandler.

"Makes you wonder if we're just as dumb as he is," Chandler said, and realized he spoke the words in his heart. Everyone could see how perfect Clark and Marlowe were. Except them. Was he just as blind?

"You don't need to wonder. Just assume yes."

Chandler laughed. His small hometown was dead serious about their patriotism and even more serious about their firearms, but they definitely knew how to not take themselves seriously, too. He missed that in Hollywood.

"Tonight we're celebrating the engagement of two people who are absolutely perfect for each other," their mother said.

Zane's voice came in his ear again, low, so only he could hear. "Funny, but she didn't say that at my engagement party."

"Mine, either. Probably for a reason, since both of our wives left us."

"I'm not falling for a pretty face again."

"Jessica wasn't that pretty," Chandler said with a smirk, talking about Zane's ex.

"Guess love is blind, 'cause I thought she was for the longest time."

"She had nice bone structure," Chandler said, using words he'd heard in Hollywood a million times. "But she didn't know how to smile. Made her ugly."

"Smiling gives you wrinkles."

"Look for a woman with wrinkles, then."

They laughed.

Whatever their mom had said had caused cheers to erupt around them. Chandler joined them, although he had no idea what, exactly he was cheering.

He watched as Clark lowered his head and kissed Marlowe, tenderly and sweetly. He'd guess, from the darkening of Marlowe's eyes, that she might be interested in a kiss with more passion. Later, probably.

"I'm not even going to think about a girl unless she looks at me just like that," Zane murmured in his ear.

Chandler nodded. "Me either."

~~~

Thanks so much for reading! **Sold! In the Show Me State** is next.

Reviews are welcome and appreciated!

Printed in Great Britain
by Amazon